SURVIVAL

LISA HARRIS

DAY ONE

CHAPTER ONE

DECEMBER 21ST

GARRETT MCQUAID LOOKED up into the barrel of the gun and knew at that moment he was going to die. But if this was his day to die, he wasn't going down without a fight.

"You pull that trigger, and you'll have the entire Shadow Ridge's police department shooting holes in your backside in the next thirty seconds." Garrett lay still and held the man's gaze while ensuring no hint of a bluff shadowed his eyes.

Elijah Duke frowned. "You're the only lawman around here, McQuaid, and you know it."

Garrett's mouth tightened. Law enforcement from the entire state had been after the Duke brothers for six days now while the two men racked up a growing list of charges. They'd tracked them all the way from a south Dallas suburb, west through Abilene, and across the dusty West Texas landscape. But while his town might not be anything more than a dot on the map on a long stretch of lonely desert, pine-covered trails, and distant snowy mountains, he'd been the one who'd picked up the men's trail.

Which meant this was going to end right here. Right now.

"If you're going to shoot me," Garrett said, "you'd better do it quickly, because you see that ridge to your right? Two deputies are coming up on that trail, just on the other side. One of them is a sharpshooter who passed with a 95 percent on his FBI pistol qualification drills. In other words, when he crests that ridge, whether I'm alive or not, you'll end up lying on the ground with a bullet in your head."

He waited for the remarks to sink in.

Elijah's gaze shifted. "I still say you're lying."

"Then how about this? I'm not ready to die. Not today, anyway."

Garrett grabbed Elijah's Glock, pushed it away from his face, and punched the man square in the jaw. The outlaw had no time to react. A fraction of a second later, Garrett grabbed the weapon with both hands, flipped Elijah onto his back, then rolled him onto his stomach.

"Still think I'm bluffing?" Garrett's boot dug into the man's backside. "Where's your brother?"

The crack of a rifle sounded in the afternoon breeze, muffling the man's answer. Garrett fell backward onto the ground. Dust blew across his face as he stared up at the sky. He couldn't move. Could barely breathe as a tightness spread across his chest. The clouds above him spun. Nausea ran through him and he could feel something wet spreading across his chest. He was losing blood. Fast. Even if someone was to find him, he was too far out to get to the clinic in town. He was going to bleed to death in this desert.

A flood of regret swept through him, followed by flashes of memory. Was this what happened when you were about to die? Segments of your life snapping into place one by one. If he did die, he knew of only one regret he'd take with him to the grave. And that was leaving behind his family. He'd married Katherine when he was only nineteen. Forty years and five children later, he'd never looked back. Never wanted anything but a quiet life in this part of the state where the reds, pinks, and blues of the sunset stretched across the desert as far as one could see, and where no one thought twice about another dust storm roaring across the skies.

But now. . .now he'd never hold his grandbabies or take that cruise he'd always promised Kat.

"Dad. . ."

Garrett heard his name and tried to speak but nothing came out. He was awake. Or at least he thought he was. He could still see the clouds hovering overhead, and if he looked hard enough, he could see Crowley's Ridge to the left. But he'd lied about the deputy sniper hiding behind the rocks. That had been a bluff.

"Dad. . .Dad, you're going to be okay. Just hang in there."

Features blurred above him.

Jace?

What was Jace doing here?

He fought to take a breath, but something was wrong.

"Dad, if you can hear me, I want you to blink."

He heard the words and fought to process them. Blink. He could do that.

"Dad." Jace pressed in closer. "Can you hear me?"

Garrett tried to answer. Time seemed to slip by in slow motion. Why couldn't he talk? Why couldn't Jace hear him? He'd blinked. Hadn't he?

Fluorescent lights glared down at him. Voices shouted.

Gunshot to the chest. Need to get him stabilized.

Get me a unit of plasma.

More white lights flickered above him, then everything went dark. He couldn't see anything, but they were shouting around him again.

"What's going on?"

"I don't know—"

"Get the power back on, now. We're losing him."

JACE MCQUAID'S father was the toughest man he knew, which meant it was going to take more than a bullet to the chest to stop him. The family patriarch had been the anchor keeping not only their family together over the past three-plus decades, but the small town of Shadow Ridge as well. But now. . .with everything that had happened in the past forty-eight hours, even his father wasn't going to be able to fix things.

Jace sat down on the edge of the bed, encouraged to see some color in his father's cheeks. "Dad. . .you're awake."

His father groaned, struggled to sit up.

"Not so fast. You were shot."

"That must be why I feel like I was the loser in a cattle stampede."

"What do you remember?" Jace asked.

"I don't know. I remember. . ." He blinked a couple times, but didn't try to sit up again. "I was out near the ridge, looking for the Duke Brothers. I turned around, and Elijah had somehow pinned me down with his weapon."

"And after that?"

"I remember seeing you. Thinking about your mother. I knew I was going to die."

"But you didn't." Jace squeezed his dad's hand, wondering when his skin had started thinning and his beard had gone completely white. "Hope said it was a miracle. Another couple inches to the left and the bullet would have hit your heart. Instead, she was able to repair the damage. Bottom line, it's going to take a while to get back to your old, ornery self, but you'll live."

"Funny, but I still don't know why you're here."

Jace shifted in his chair. "You don't remember?"

His father's brow narrowed as he searched for the elusive answer to Jace's question before finally shaking his head.

"Tess, Levi, and I drove into town for your fortieth anniversary Thursday afternoon." Jace felt a fresh wave of emotion hit. "We had a family dinner at Morgan's Diner that night, and were supposed to have a big party Friday night. Do you remember anything?"

"Your mom ordered lemon meringue pie. It's always been her favorite."

Jace's smile quickly faded. "I heard you were out looking for the Duke brothers Friday morning. Alone. I went out to find you."

"They got away?"

"Actually, they're in custody, but there is something else." Jace paused before continuing. "Do you know what an EMP is?"

"Of course. It stands for. . .electricity. . .something."

Concern over his father's confusion deepened, but Hope had said that would pass. It had to. "It's an electromagnetic pulse, and if one were to strike, it would do an insurmountable amount of damage. From the electric grid, to telecommunications, to infrastructure. Stoplights would go down, airplanes couldn't fly, there would be no internet."

His father's eyes narrowed. "Why are you telling me this, Jace?"

"We can't be a hundred percent sure at this point, but we think one struck here."

"You're telling me the grid is down?"

"Yes, though right now we're not sure why or how. It could

have been from a nuclear weapon or massive solar flare. But everything's been affected. There's no internet, no cell phones, and power lines are down." Jace's jaw tensed. "There were also a number of car accidents when it happened."

His dad glanced around the room. The monitors at his bedside weren't on. No buzzing of overhead lights or hum of an air-conditioner. No sounds of traffic from the open window. The quiet was unnerving.

His dad grabbed the bed rail. "I need to get up."

"You're not going anywhere. The only reason you're alive is because the clinic's emergency generators kicked in while you were on the operating table."

"So what are you doing?"

"We've been going door-to-door telling people what's going on. Trying to make sure no one panics. Problem is, there's a good chance there won't be any transport trucks coming through anytime soon. All I know to do is encourage people to ration their goods and help out their neighbors."

"There's got to be news on the radio."

"Not yet. I've been waiting for information, but so far, there's nothing. A few people have driven to neighboring towns, but we still don't know if the strike hit a hundred square miles, or the entire country." Saying it out loud somehow punctuated the reality of the situation. "We don't know if we're looking at a week without electricity, or a year."

"How long has it been?"

"Almost two days. We've prioritized the gas in town for essentials, like the clinic, but we don't know how much longer we'll be able to run the generator."

"People are going to die, Jace."

His jaw tensed and he shifted his gaze to the tiled floor. "People already have."

"Where's your mother?"

Jace caught the panic in his father's voice. "Dad, right now, I need you to focus on getting better—"

His dad pulled back the sheet. "Tell me where she is, Jace."

"You can't get up—"

"Tell me where she is."

His lungs constricted. He couldn't tell his father the truth. Not now. He might be the strongest person he knew, but this. . . . This was going to destroy him.

His father grabbed Jace's hand. "Tell me what happened to your mother."

"She. . ." Jace fought the overwhelming surge of emotion. "She was heading back to the ranch when it happened. She was hit by a semi on Waters Road. She died on impact."

"No. You're wrong. This can't be happening." His dad yanked at the IV in his arm.

"Dad, stop." Jace grabbed his father's hands and squeezed them together. "I know this is a lot to take in, but right now, my only concern is your getting well."

"I don't care about that. She can't be dead. When I got the call about the Duke brothers I promised her I'd be back in plenty of time to celebrate our anniversary."

Jace fought back the tears. "I'm sorry, Dad. So, so sorry."

"Hope did my surgery?"

Jace nodded.

"What about Tess?"

"She and Levi are out at the ranch, taking care of things."

"What about Sam?"

Jace shook his head, not sure how much bad news his father was going to be able to take. "He was planning to be here for your party, but hadn't gotten here yet."

"So he's missing."

"I'm sure he's fine," Jace rushed on. "We know of dozens of

people still missing. Some of them are just now starting to show up. He'll show up, Dad."

"People are going to start panicking, and Chase. . .Chase might be a great deputy, but he can't handle all of this by himself. You have experience, Jace. Until I'm back on my feet, I'm going to need you to step up and protect this town from whatever's going on."

Jace stood and turned toward the window, watching as a red-tailed hawk circled in the distance. How was he supposed to tell his father that the town's one officer under him, Chase Beckett, had been transferring prisoners when the grid went down and was now also missing?

Jace's jaw tensed. Or that he had no intention of ever putting a badge on again.

An unexpected shiver slipped through him. He'd returned to Shadow Ridge to celebrate his parents' fortieth anniversary, with plans of leaving right after Christmas. But his father was right about one thing. The panic had already begun—looting in stores, fights breaking out over supplies, and already a string of break-ins. And that was just after forty-eight hours. How long would it take until things spiraled completely out of control?

He glanced back at his father. No electricity, no internet, and no modern technology or access to forensic labs. Not only was he the only law in town, he was going to have to learn how to fight crime all over again.

DAY 264

CHAPTER TWO

SEPTEMBER 10TH

JACE STUFFED his hands into the pockets of his jacket as he made the short walk from his small house on Bowen Avenue, past a row of empty storefronts, toward the brick-faced police department on Main Street. While no one knew yet what had caused the blackout—or the Quake as most called it because of the rumbling vibrations felt across the valley that afternoon—everyone had struggled through their first summer without electricity in the hot west Texas climate. Thirty-three hadn't survived.

And they weren't the only ones.

The day before the Quake the population of Shadow Ridge was seven hundred and forty-two people. Nine months later, he estimated just over five hundred. He knew because he had been the one who made a list of every person who had died. Before long, a covered wall outside city hall had a growing number of photos, not only of those the town had lost, but those who were still missing. Like his brother Sam and Chase, his sister's high school sweetheart she'd recently reconnected with.

Along with the deep-rooted loss had come just as many questions. Rumors had started circulating from day one. Some said the Russians had attacked with a nuclear bomb. Others said the Chinese had hit the country with EMP bursts, while still others claimed it had to have been a solar flare. All Jace really knew was the impact. No internet or electricity, a serious food crisis, and no way to communicate with the rest of the world.

Immediately after the grid went down, they'd tried to get answers to those questions by sending out scouts, but the information they'd been able to bring back was nominal, and the risk had proven substantial. Armed gangs and other organized crime groups taking advantage of the situation had made travel across the region dangerous. And the lack of news from the outside world made the secluded town of Shadow Ridge feel even more isolated.

Jace paused for a second in front of the Hartz Movie Theater. No one had bothered to change the marquee above the entrance that still promoted an Alfred Hitchcock marathon weekend. That had been the last time Fred Cooper had opened the theater. Reminders of the Quake were everywhere—from rows of empty shops to the dozens of undrivable cars scattered throughout the town. But the Quake and everything that followed had not only stolen normalcy of life, it had brought with it an overwhelming grief in very personal ways.

On top of losing his mother, Jace had watched his father go from a vibrant father of five, ready to celebrate four decades of marriage to the love of his life, to a man he hardly knew anymore. Nerve damage from the bullet had caused a loss of mobility in his left leg that had left him with a noticeable limp.

But there had been little time to grieve. The townspeople had voted early on that he and his younger brother Levi, the only ones in town with law enforcement experience, take over until their father was back on his feet. Or until things got back to normal. It hadn't mattered that Jace was only visiting after having just left the military or that Levi had just graduated from the police training academy and hadn't completed his field training. Both of them had reluctantly agreed. But Jace never expected to still be here almost a year later.

Shadow Ridge had always been one of those undiscovered towns in the middle of blue skies, tumbleweeds, and distant mountain ranges. A place that was never the destination but simply a mile marker on the journey. Because of it, people missed what the town had to offer. Like some of the best roadside barbecue in the state, Fourth of July parades with watermelon and ice cream, and night skies that made you feel as if you could reach out and touch the stars. But now, Morgan's diner had closed down, the Bluebell ice cream in Grady's grocery store freezers gone, and people had been too busy surviving to think about a holiday.

The only thing that hadn't changed was the stars and the sun that never failed to rise.

They'd turned the library into a gathering place where people shared knowledge about making soap, building smokehouses, and planting root vegetables in preparation for winter. Some of the women had planted herbs and created a small exchange store where people could come for things they needed and donate things they didn't. Because money was worthless and most of the medicine in the hospital and pharmacy had been wiped out weeks ago, they'd turned to utilizing herbs for wounds and sicknesses and learning everything they could about survival.

But Jace's fear was that with the dwindling population of the town—and dwindling access to supplies—winter was going to hit hard.

"Jace?"

Pulled out of his thoughts, he turned around and smiled at the familiar face. "Morgan. I was planning to come by your place later today. Jules McIntyre gave me some new seeds. I thought you might be able to use them in the greenhouses."

He stopped, noticing her usual smile was gone and that she wasn't really listening. Which wasn't like her. Morgan had lost her husband during the Quake, leaving her to raise her six-year-old son by herself. In the last nine months, he'd learned she was one of the strongest people he knew.

But today he caught a noticeable panic in her dark eyes.

"Morgan, what's wrong?"

"It's Noah."

"Have the kids been bullying him again?"

"No, not since you showed up and gave them all a piece of your mind." Her gaze flicked to the left. "You've done so much for us already that I hate to bother you with anything else, but—"

"It's fine. What happened?"

"I know this is going to sound strange, but Noah saw something this morning."

"Saw something?" Jace set his hands on his hips. "What do you mean?"

"That's the problem. I don't know. He was out looking for rabbits this morning with this new slingshot Gavin Pikes gave him. I told him not to go far, but you know Noah. He tends to lose track of time and wanders."

"He's lost?"

"No. He came home." She drew in a deep breath. "He hasn't said a word since. He just sits and stares out the window. He won't talk. He wouldn't eat his breakfast."

Jace frowned. He'd never known Noah not to have something to say.

"He hasn't said anything at all?"

"No."

"Where is he now?"

"I left him at the library with Margaret while I came to find you. I thought. . .I don't know. I thought maybe you knew about something that had happened this morning. Something he might've seen."

As tensions rose across the town from the lack of food and resources, crime had also gone up significantly. Primarily petty crime, the occasional assault and too-frequent burglaries. But in a small town like Shadow Ridge, where everyone knew everyone, any crime felt personal. Thankfully, today had been quiet so far, as he finished his early morning rounds.

Morgan brushed a dark strand of hair back from her eyes and caught his gaze. "I know my boy, Jace. Something's wrong. He saw something."

"Okay. . ." His mind clicked through the list of options of how to proceed. "I think we should take him to see Hope."

"I thought about that, but she's overloaded with work, and he's not sick—"

"I understand, but you know my sister. She has a way with people—kids in particular—and she's had to do a lot of trauma counseling on top of her doctoring over the past few months. Maybe she can get him to talk."

He caught the doubt in Morgan's eyes, but he'd seen his sister at work. As the town's only doctor, she'd been forced to step up and deal with not just physical issues, but emotional and psychological trauma as well—because the fallout from the Quake had gone far beyond just the physical repercussions. Everyone in the town had been affected in one way or another, and her workload had dramatically increased.

"Do you trust me?" he asked.

Morgan's jaw tensed, fear still present in her eyes, but she nodded. "I trust both of you, but that doesn't take away the panic."

"Go get Noah and meet me at the clinic."

Five minutes later, the bell jingled above the door as Jace stepped into the clinic located a block away from the police department. Before the Quake, patients needing advanced medical care were typically either life-flighted or driven by ambulance to the nearest county hospital seventy-five miles away. Sometimes, like after his father being shot, they used the clinic to stabilize a victim. Now, there was no way to transport a patient, which meant that everything from a runny nose to cardiac arrest had to be taken care of here.

"Hey, Doc. You here?" Jace walked through the empty waiting room and past reception toward his sister's office. "I've got this rash. . ."

"Take a number." She stepped out of her office and shot him an amused look. "In case you didn't know, half the town has a rash, or a fungus, or some kind of cruddy cough, and I'm down to the last few doses of antibiotics and pain medicine."

"What about the medicinal plant garden you're working on. How's it coming?"

Hope brushed passed him, grabbed a stack of charts off the reception counter, and headed toward the filing cabinet. He was pretty sure she never stopped working. "At eighty-five, Fannie's a wealth of information and has more energy than people half her age. Which means between her and the library information we've compiled, most of the plants are thriving. But it takes time. In the meantime, both of my nurses are out today, leaving me to see patients, file these charts, and—"

"You shouldn't be doing this." He grabbed the charts out of her hands and set them down. "I've told you to train a couple people to help pick up the slack. You can't keep up this pace."

Hope had gone to med school then decided to return to

Shadow Ridge last year when Dr. Goodman retired. After rekindling a relationship with Chase, she thought she'd settle down with him and run the small clinic. But dreams don't always come true. Everyone had been affected by the Quake, and Hope was no exception.

She dropped her hands to her sides. "I don't have a lot of options, Jace. Karen comes in three mornings a week, and Mrs. Carlson is coming in the other two days to keep up with the paperwork. The problem is people have to provide for their families, and we don't exactly make a living here."

"What about Tess?"

"She comes twice a week, but Dad still needs her."

He understood Hope's reluctance. Tess had always been a free spirit. She was the risk-taker of the family, content to march to her own drum. And even though she might not show it, losing her mother at nineteen had devastated her.

"She needs a project," Jace said. "She's still grieving losing Mom—"

"I know." Hope grabbed the charts Jace had taken from her and started filing them in the cabinet. "I've tried talking to her about it, but she shuts me down every time."

"I know, and I'm sorry. I'm not trying to lay it back on you. I know you've taken on far more than most people in this town."

"But look what I get in return." She pointed to a plastic sack leaning against the wall that was filled with what looked like some kind of vegetable.

"What is that?" Jace asked.

"A payment from Caroline. Apparently, she had a bumper crop of eggplant she just harvested. And you should see my backyard. I've got a second goat and three more chickens." She slipped in the last file then slid the drawer shut. "People are going to start showing up in about fifteen minutes, and I'm assuming you're not here for a social visit."

"Something we don't do often enough."

Her expression softened. "I know."

In trying to keep things as normal as possible, Jace had tried to make it to the weekly Sunday meal at the ranch, but the empty chair at the table was a painful reminder. Katherine McQuaid had been the cement that held the family together. Without her, it seemed as if they were all floundering.

"It's Morgan," he said, pushing away those thoughts.

"Morgan?" She caught her brother's gaze. "What happened?"

"It's Noah, actually."

"If he's sick, she needs to bring him in."

Jace hesitated. "Morgan thinks he saw something this morning. Something that might have traumatized him."

"Like what?"

"I'm not sure, but you know Morgan better than anyone. She's not prone to hysterics. And if he did see something. . ."

"You need to know."

Jace nodded. "He won't talk. Won't respond to her. Something happened."

"Okay. Have her come in as soon as possible."

"She's on her way with him now. I hope that's okay."

Hope folded her arms across her chest. "Of course, though I might have to have you sign up to volunteer if you're going to start bringing me patients."

He kissed her on the cheek and shot her a smile. "I owe you, little sister."

"Yes, you do."

She turned away, but not before Jace caught her blinking back tears.

"Hey. . . Are you okay?"

"Yes." She wiped her eyes before turning back to him. "It's nothing. Really."

"Why don't I believe that?"

"I'm trying to keep things in perspective. So many people have lost someone." She glanced down at her ringless hand. "At least I have the hope that he's alive, but today is Chase's birthday. He's thirty-two, and I. . .I still don't know where he is."

He caught his sister's hand and squeezed it. "I'm sorry."

"I know." She nodded. "Seeing him again last fall seems almost surreal. Sometimes I wonder if I just dreamed it. It seems like a lifetime ago."

"I haven't stopped believing that both he and Sam are still out there, trying to get back home."

"Me too. Some days are just harder than others."

The knot in his gut tightened. Small gangs of looters had formed over the past nine months, making travel from one town to the next dangerous, keeping Shadow Ridge primarily in the dark. And keeping the missing from coming home.

The front bell jingled again.

"Morgan's here," Hope said.

She wiped her eyes again and smiled, but he didn't miss the fatigue in her expression. And he couldn't blame her. Most days he felt as if he was just waiting for the next inevitable crisis. And if his gut was right, another one was about to hit.

CHAPTER THREE

MORGAN SQUEEZED Noah's hand as they stepped into the one-story complex that had been built back in the early seventies by a generous grant from one of the town's founding fathers. Noah had been born in this clinic, and it was where she'd always brought him for checkups, vaccinations, and bouts of the flu. Before the Quake, like many rural medical facilities, it had struggled to stay afloat, and a lack of capital made it difficult to keep up with technology. Because Hope was the only physician within a seventy-five mile radius, the town's reliance on her and her medical knowledge had increased exponentially.

Morgan kissed Noah on the top of his head. "Why don't you go sit for a minute at the table and read a book. I'll be right back. I promise. I'm just going to talk with Hope for a minute."

Noah didn't respond. He just went and sat down. Morgan walked across the room to where Jace and Hope stood, not wanting her son to hear their conversation.

Hope gave her a hug, then took a step back. "Jace said he won't talk."

"I hope I don't sound crazy, but I don't know what to do."

Morgan shook her head. "You know Noah. He's normally a chatterbox, and I can't get him to be quiet, but he came in from playing this morning and. . . You can see him. I've always tried not to be overprotective and worry all the time, but it's like he's not there. Something happened."

"A mother's instincts are usually right," Hope said, squeezing Morgan's hand. "We're going to find out what happened. I promise."

Morgan nodded, trying to stuff down the fear bubbling inside her, but it was impossible to quell.

"I have an idea," Hope said. "Does he still like to draw?"

"He's gone through just about every piece of paper we have in the house. I'm not sure what I'm going to do when they're gone or his markers dry up."

Hope reached behind the receptionist's desk and pulled out a couple sheets of paper and a box of crayons. "On top of whatever happened today, we have to remember he's been through a lot the past few months."

"You think this is some delayed reaction?" Morgan asked.

"Not necessarily. I'm just saying the stress can build up over time and come out when we least expect it."

"I should have been watching for something like this—"

Hope shook her head. "Morgan, I'm not saying any of this to make you feel guilty.

We're all doing what we have to do simply to survive. And you're doing an incredible job. Don't ever forget that."

Morgan nodded, but months of living on the edge had left her exhausted most days and always second-guessing her parenting of an overly adventurous boy who'd lost his father. There hadn't even been time to properly grieve. The town had buried their dead, then immediately switched to survival mode. Hours had quickly turned into days, which had turned into weeks, then months, with no end in sight. No electricity. No clean water. She'd gone from running the town's diner to taking over her husband's greenhouses, raising rabbits and chickens, and learning how to preserve a harvest without electricity. All in order to feed her child.

Morgan forced her mind to focus. "Noah, Dr. Hope would like to talk to you."

Noah didn't respond.

Morgan sat down next to her son on one of the small plastic chairs, while Hope took the one on the other side. Jace leaned back against the receptionist's desk, out of the way.

"I have something for you, Noah." Hope slipped the paper in front of him along with the small box of crayons. "I save these for my favorite patients."

Noah just stared at the paper.

"I wondered if you'd like to draw with me?" she continued, picking out a purple crayon.

There was still no response from Noah.

"I heard you like rabbits." She started drawing on the corner of the paper. A face. Long ears. Whiskers. And then a body. "Did you know that I had never eaten a rabbit until a few months ago?"

Still nothing.

"I was sure I wouldn't like rabbit stew, but you know what? Now I love rabbit stew, squirrel stew, and even venison stew."

"I like rabbit stew," said Noah. "My mom's tastes the best."

Hope smiled at the response. "I've had your mom's stew. More than once. And you're right. It is the best."

"But she lets me keep Thumper as a pet and promised me she won't cook him."

"I always wanted a pet rabbit. Instead, my mom taught me how to draw bunnies." Hope drew another rabbit.

"Where is she?"

"My mother?" Hope glanced at Morgan before responding.

Morgan had talked to Noah about death when his father had died, but guiding a six-year-old through the maze of loss was overwhelming. It wasn't just the fact that Tommy was gone and she was a widow. In an instant, everything normal had vanished.

She nodded at Hope, knowing Noah couldn't be sheltered from what was going on around them.

"My mother died," Hope said.

"My daddy died too."

"I know. You must miss him."

Noah picked up one of the crayons before dropping it back onto the table and staring at it.

"Would you like to draw something?" Hope asked.

Noah hesitated, then shifted and reached for a red crayon. Morgan felt her breath catch as her son started drawing a figure. He was lying on the ground in a puddle of blood.

"Wow, you're quite the artist," Hope said.

Morgan rested her arm across the back of her son's chair, her stomach tied in knots.

Hope put her crayon down. "Noah, can you tell me about what you drew?"

"I saw a man."

"When you were out looking for rabbits?"

Noah nodded.

"Can you tell me about the man in the picture?" Hope asked. "Was he hurt?"

Noah nodded again. "He wasn't moving. There was blood. Lots of blood on his head."

"That had to be scary. You know my brother who's standing over there?" Hope pointed to Jace. "You know what he does?"

Hope motioned for Jace to sit down beside them at the table.

"He helps people," Noah said.

"Exactly. He helps people who are hurt. And he tries to keep our town safe."

"He comes to my house sometimes," Noah said. "He brings my mom seeds. Sometimes he brings her food like Miss Margaret's raspberry jam."

"I'm not surprised." Hope smiled. "He likes taking care of people. And this picture that you drew. . . If someone is in trouble, he needs to help him."

Morgan pulled Noah against her and felt her heart break. No six-year-old should have to see the things her son had seen. She'd always been strict about video games and television, and yet in real life, he'd seen far more than he ever should have. And now, if he'd seen someone who was hurt . .

Jace took off his cowboy hat, set it on the table, then pulled his chair a few inches closer to Noah. "Do you mind if I ask you a couple of questions?"

Noah shook his head.

"Where did you see the man?" Jace asked.

"He was in the warehouse, where people keep the food. I was. . .chasing a rabbit."

"Good." Jace hesitated before asking another question. "Did you see who hurt the man?"

"No. But I. . ." Noah pressed his lips together. "Before I went into the warehouse. . .I heard a gunshot."

Morgan felt her breath catch at her son's admission.

"Did you see anyone?" Jace asked.

"No."

Jace tousled Noah's hair. "It was brave of you to tell us what you saw. Thank you."

"Are you going to find who hurt him?" Noah asked.

"I'm going to do everything I can," Jace said. "I know what you saw was scary. I see a lot of scary things too. But you did the right thing. And you know what?"

"What?"

"If it's okay with your mom, I'd like to come see you later." Jace leaned forward. "Because I have some licorice."

"Really?" Noah's eyes brightened for the first time. "You have licorice?"

"I heard you like it, but. . ." Jace put his finger to his lips. "Don't tell anyone."

A familiar smile lingered on her son's face for a few seconds. That's what she needed to see. To know that her little boy was still in there.

"Why don't you keep coloring with Dr. Hope," Jace said, "while I talk to your mom for a minute?"

"Grown-up talk?" Noah rolled his eyes but kept coloring.

Jace grinned back at him. "You're a smart kid."

Morgan stepped away from the table with him, trying not to feel the growing panic.

"I need you to think again," Jace said, touching her elbow. "Did you hear any gunshots, or something that might have sounded like shots this morning?"

"No." A sinking feeling settled in her stomach. "I'm sorry."

"It's okay. I just need to establish some kind of timeline to all of this." He leaned against the counter. "I'm going back to the office to get Levi before I go out there, but I want you to promise me that you and Noah will stay in town until we know what's going on. Somewhere like the library or town hall where lots of people are coming and going."

Morgan shook her head. "We'll be fine. I haven't let anything that's happened yet scare me away, and I don't intend to start running now."

His frown deepened at her response. "You wouldn't be running away. Just keeping yourself safe until I come back."

She shot him a smile, trying to dispel the tension between them. "Do you worry about all the single women in town as much as you worry about me?"

Morgan caught the surprise in Jace's eyes and immediately regretted her flippant response.

"I'm sorry, I. . ." She fumbled with her words, trying to backtrack. He wasn't flirting with her. He was just doing his job.

"I just need you to be safe," he said. "We don't know exactly what Noah saw or if someone saw him. It's possible that he saw more than he's telling us. Just promise me."

The fear in her gut she'd fought for so long had settled back again. "You think someone might come after him? Someone who knows what he saw?"

"It's a possibility we can't ignore."

Morgan glanced back at Noah. She might say she could handle things on her own, but she wasn't going to do anything that could potentially risk the life of her son. "I'll do what you said, but I'm not the only one who needs to be careful."

Jace nodded. "I'll let you know what we find as soon as I can."

A moment later, the door shut behind him.

"Morgan?"

She turned back to Hope, who got up from the table.

"I was just getting ready to eat some breakfast before the clinic opened," she said. "I could use some company if the two of you are hungry."

"Hope, you don't have to—"

"Of course, I don't have to, but one, you're my best friend, and two, I've got oatmeal and blueberries, thanks to Mrs. Fisher."

Morgan forced a smile. Hope had inherited the same stubbornness as her brother. “What do you say, champ?”

Noah shrugged. “Okay.”

Hope pulled her into a hug. “Jace will figure out what’s going on.”

Morgan nodded, but what if her son had witnessed a murder? And what if someone out there knew it?

CHAPTER FOUR

JACE TRIED to get Levi on his solar-powered radio as he hurried down Main Street, but couldn't get a response. Having a two person police department was common in the small towns scattered across the western expanse of the state. For as long as he could remember, his dad had been the police chief in Shadow Ridge, most of the time with only one officer under him. That meant that not only did Garrett McQuaid have to be available at any hour of the day, but he was also in charge of patrol, traffic, investigations. . .everything. Jace had promised himself since high school he would never be in his dad's position. And yet, here he was, trying to protect an entire town with little to no resources. At least his father could call the county sheriff in the next town over and get back up. Jace couldn't even do that.

Do you worry about all the single women as much as you worry about me?

Morgan's pointed question had thrown him off, because he knew the answer. Her calm spirit and service to the community had showed a deep commitment not just to her son but to those around her. But none of that mattered. He silenced the train of thought. Her husband had died nine months ago, and on top of that, he had his own reasons for not pursuing a relationship. He had a town to protect.

Jace stepped into the small lobby of the police department. "Levi? You here?"

"I'm in the office."

"I've been trying to get you on the radio—" Jace stopped in the doorway. "Mrs. Robinson, is everything okay?"

"It's Clark." Sunlight from the window lit up the room as the older woman pulled her purse against her chest and frowned. "I heard his car leave last night, just after midnight, and your brother here. . .he refuses to go look for him."

Levi held up his hands. "That's not true, Mrs. Robinson. I've been trying to explain that—"

"So help me, if he went off with that girl who works at the drugstore. That man's about as sharp as a bowl of mashed potatoes."

"Mrs. Robinson—"

"Don't try to argue with me, Levi McQuaid. I pay my taxes every year, and a hefty percentage of that goes into your paycheck. That means you work for me. And I want you out looking for Clark before he gets himself into trouble." She tilted her head, gray curls that had always been stark black until the last few months, her jaw set as if she were about to pounce on both of them. "If your father were here, I wouldn't be having this conversation."

Levi let out a sharp breath. "Mrs. Robinson, I've been trying to tell you that—"

"Stop trying to change the subject, young man. I thought your mama raised you better than that. Your attitude comes across as discourteous and insolent."

"I'm sorry." Levi glanced at Jace. "Help me here, big brother."

Jace leaned against the doorframe. He'd lost count of how

many times he'd had this same conversation with the woman. He felt his heart break.

Mrs. Robinson set her purse down, then picked up the photo on the desk. Her brow furrowed as she ran her finger across the glass. "How is your mama? I can't even remember the last time I saw her. . ."

Her voice trailed off as confusion clouded her expression, then her eyes widened as realization hit her. She glanced back at the photo, then at the stalled fan above them that hadn't worked for months.

"Clark isn't coming back, is he?" she whispered. "He's gone. Just like your mother."

Jace knelt down in front of the woman and shook his head. "I'm so sorry. I know you miss him. We all do, but no. He's not coming back."

"Sometimes. . .sometimes I want him here so bad that I forget what happened." Mrs. Robinson sat back in the chair, her jaw slack. "I go to sleep, praying I'll wake up in the morning and he'll be lying beside me like he did for fifty-plus years."

"I know this is hard. Can I take you back home, or to your daughter's?" Jace asked.

"No. I'll be okay."

"I really don't mind."

She reached up and touched his cheek before standing up. "You're a sweet boy, Jace McQuaid. I wish your mother could see you now. She'd be proud."

Jace watched her leave the room, wishing he could ignore the ache in his chest.

"I don't know how you do that." Levi's statement broke through his thoughts. "When I talk to her, I just end up going in circles and frustrating both of us. She makes me dizzy."

"She's good at that. And it's not you. You're doing a great job, little brother." Jace's smile quickly faded.

"What's wrong?" Levi asked.

Jace picked his backpack up off the desk. "We need to head out to the warehouse."

"What's going on?"

"We have a witness who saw a dead man there."

Levi frowned. "Who was your witness?"

Jace grabbed a couple rifles from the locked gun safe, hesitating before answering.

"Jace?"

"Morgan Addison's son, Noah."

"Wait a minute." His brother took a step away from the desk. "Morgan's son is what? Six or seven years old?"

"Yes, but he said he saw a dead man inside the warehouse."

"What was he doing out there?"

"The warehouse isn't far from their house. He was looking for rabbit for dinner."

"Did Morgan hear any gunshots?"

"No."

"Did it ever occur to you that he might have made up the story so he wouldn't get into trouble for, I don't know. . .wandering off?"

Jace turned back around and set the weapons on the desk before locking the cabinet again. "You didn't see him, Levi. He definitely saw something. At the least, we need to check it out."

"I agree, I just feel like I've been doing a lot of interventions. You'd think people could act like grown men and women instead of six-year-olds. Actually, I give Noah more credit than some of the adults around here."

"People have been acting irresponsibly for as long as I can remember, and everything that's happened just multiplies that. Think of it as job security, little brother."

Levi let out a laugh. "Except now I get paid with chickens and surprise pies."

"The navy bean pie was a little over the top." Jace handed Levi one of the shotguns then did a quick safety check. "I don't think he's making this up."

Which means they could be looking at a murder.

Jace and Levi saddled up Brisket and Cactus, two of the horses from their father's ranch they now kept in town at a converted stable next to the police station.

"Where's your radio?" Jace asked as he swung up onto Brisket.

"Sorry about that. I think my solar charger's dying. No matter how long I leave it out there, it's hit-and-miss."

Jace frowned. He was grateful for the limited solar technology and power banks they'd been able to source, but they still took significantly longer to charge, and even in full sun it could easily take over twenty-four hours to fully charge their devices.

The old warehouse sat on the edge of town in the middle of a field of blue gamma. It had been decided by unanimous vote to use the large building to store food for the community for the coming winter. The back of the property had been tilled and fertilized and was used for the community garden. Volunteers were scheduled to work five-hour shifts during the day, and armed guards were set up in shifts around the perimeter at night to ensure no one stole the food. They'd established limits as to how much each household could take every month, with priority given to the elderly and infirm, and so far the system had worked well.

One of the greatest sources of information the past few months had been Otis Crawley. He'd grown up on a homestead with no electricity or running water and could still remember his mother plucking chickens for Sunday dinner, making her own homemade soap, and washing clothes in the riverbank. A year ago, no one in Shadow Ridge could've imagined doing any of those things. But nothing was the same as it had been a year ago.

Along with Otis, several farmers had also come forward to share their knowledge on growing drought-tolerant corn, animal feed, and peanuts. Teams had been formed to create solar dehydration systems, springhouses, zero-energy coolers, beehives, and smokehouses. They'd further insulated greenhouses and built trellises and shade coverings, all set up in an effort to combat—and utilize—the west Texas sun.

And their hard work was paying off.

They'd developed a strategy that had both built community and shared resources and knowledge, giving Jace faith that its implementation would save the town in the months to come. But he didn't miss the irony of the situation. Minus a scattering of broken-down cars, it could be a hundred years ago with the law in town still riding horses and wearing cowboy hats.

"You look tired," Jace said, breaking the quiet between them.

Levi shrugged. "I didn't get a lot of sleep last night. I'm still convinced you somehow have a hand in this. I think you're paying people to wake me up at night."

It had become a running joke. Levi always seemed to get called out on the nights when he was on duty, while Jace typically managed to sleep through his shifts with no calls.

"Who was it this time?" Jace asked.

"Carl Schmidt."

Jace chuckled. "The accountant?"

"It's not funny. He's completely paranoid. He comes by at least once a week either with complaints about his wife or a neighbor. . ."

Jace waited for his brother to continue, not even trying to mask his amusement as they approached the warehouse.

"He showed up at the station at two," Levi said.

"And. . ."

"I went and checked out his complaint. This time he was right. Someone had broken in through his back door."

"Was anything missing?"

"Not that he could determine in the dark. Someone shattered the window, but the intruder must've gotten spooked and run. I told him I'd come back when it was daylight."

Something moved on the far side of the building.

Jace motioned with his hand but didn't speak. He quickly dismounted, tied Brisket to a nearby fence post, then pulled out his weapon. A rabbit ran out of the barn, startling both of them.

This time Levi was the one to laugh at the surprise intruder. "Are you sure that isn't what Noah saw?"

Jace slid open the large double door that was slightly ajar and stepped inside. Sunlight hit the cement floor where a body lay. He took another step forward. A man lay on the warehouse floor, shot in the head, execution style.

CHAPTER FIVE

"So, Noah was right."

Sunlight streamed through the doorway, casting rays of light across the cement floor of the large warehouse. Jace's jaw tightened as he crouched down beside the body, immediately recognizing Jeremiah Daniels. He looked for signs of struggle on the man's hands and arms. There was no evidence of a fight. No scratches or bruising.

What had happened here?

Jeremiah Daniels and Frank Savage had been the ones in charge of storing food for the town for the past seven months —two of many good men in the community who not only worked day and night to provide for their own families, but also to ensure the community at large survived. Without men like them, this town would have turned into a ghost town months ago. But now. . .

"Cause of death seems pretty obvious to me," Levi said. "A shot in the back of the head."

Jace stood up and slowly turned in a circle while he studied the scene. The warehouse was used both as storage for the community's food and for animal feed for the livestock. They'd laid freezers and old refrigerators on their sides to use as storage facilities, along with heavy-duty IBC tanks for the grain.

"But then where's Frank?" Jace looked over at his brother, who stood with his hands at

his side, face pale in the early morning sunlight. "Frank—like Jeremiah—took his responsibility to the town seriously and never missed a shift."

"He could be in trouble."

Jace nodded, but they were both going to have to stay objective in order to unravel what had happened here. His brother was trained in an array of skills and defensive tactics, but the emotional skills that were also essential took time to acquire. Today's on-the-job training was something no one wanted to experience.

They took the next five minutes to search the perimeter of the property, but there was no sign of Frank. Only tracks leading from the warehouse to the main road.

"Can you tell how much food is missing?" Jace asked, as they walked back into the warehouse.

"I was out here yesterday morning," Levi said. "I'd guess at least three or four of the IBC tanks are missing."

Several tracks lead from the middle of the room to the door, but dozens of people came through here every day, leaving clusters of footprints across the warehouse floor. Narrowing down a suspect that way would be impossible. Jeremiah probably hadn't even known what hit him. Jace let out a sharp breath. On the surface, Levi's conclusion seemed spot on. Someone had come, shot Jeremiah, then left with as much food as they could transport.

"With Frank and Jeremiah out of the way," Levi said, turning back to his brother, "it would have been easy to load things onto a wagon and disappear into the darkness."

Jace slowly searched the crime scene in a spiral pattern, working his way outward while he looked for anything that might give them further insight into what had happened. A sprinkle of red on the cement floor fifteen feet away from the body stopped him in his tracks.

"Levi," he said, crouching down beside it. "This looks like blood."

His brother stepped up next to him. "I agree, but that shot would have killed Jeremiah instantly, and there's no sign that his body has been moved."

"Good observation," Jace said, pulling out an evidence marker from his backpack. "Then whose blood is this?"

"Maybe Frank. Maybe our shooter's?" Levi shoved his hands into his back pockets. "We can't ignore the possibility that this might have been an inside job. Not only was Frank's garden not producing like he'd hoped, several of his animals were sick. He was worried about winter coming."

"Along with every person in this town." Jace frowned. "But it's true that everything stolen would sell for a high price on the black market."

As far as he knew, no permanent location had been set up where illegal and stolen goods were being traded, but drugs, tobacco, and moonshine were readily available. Which was the reason they had put security teams in place—something that clearly hadn't been enough.

"How are we supposed to do this?" Levi threw his hands up in defeat. ""We can't exactly dust for fingerprints or put out a BOLO. And I've never had to investigate a murder scene."

No, but Jace had.

Jace shoved back the memories he'd tried so long to escape. The image of twisted metal and bodies forever imprinted in his mind. But Levi had a point. This. . .this was like working in the dark.

Jace refocused his thoughts and continued the search. He stopped again as the smell of tobacco, laced with licorice and fruit, filled his nostrils. "Do you know if either man chewed tobacco?"

"Do you really think that's important?" Levi asked. "Charlie Rand makes his own tobacco and sells it, but it could have been anyone."

"We can't dismiss anything, no matter how insignificant," Jace said. "Right now, I need you to go get Tess. We need her to do some sketches of the scene."

"Isn't your phone charged?"

"Yes, and I'll take photos, but just like you worry about your radio, I'm worried that one of these days I won't be able to access what I have on it anymore."

"Then Tess is a good idea," Levi said.

"Go ahead and talk to Frank's wife on your way back. Don't tell her what happened yet, but find out if he went into work last night and when she saw him last."

"What are you going to do?"

"Finish processing the scene and make sure we didn't miss anything before people start showing up." Jace stopped. "As soon as I'm done here, I'll go talk with Jeremiah's wife, and then it looks like we might have to put together a search party for Frank."

Jace was making a second sweep of the scene when Tess walked into the warehouse, the handle of her art satchel clenched in her hand. His sister had tied her long hair into a single braid down her back and was wearing jean shorts with a flowy shirt and sandals. Tess had always been unconventional, passionate, and creative. But the last nine months had put a damper on her spirit, enough that Jace was worried about her.

He watched as her gaze snapped from him to the body on the floor, then froze.

"What happened?" she asked.

"That's what we're trying to find out. Jeremiah was shot last night while on duty."

Tess's leather satchel fell to the ground, spilling papers, notebooks, and pencils across the sawdust floor. "He's dead?"

Jace walked to where she stood. "I'm sorry, I thought Levi would've told you."

"He said someone had been shot, but I thought. . ." She didn't finish her sentence. "I can't do this."

Tess turned and started running, stumbling on a rock. She caught her balance then disappeared around the side of the warehouse.

"Tess!" Jace took off after her. He shouldn't have been so insensitive. Should have known that she couldn't handle something like this. He'd gotten so caught up in what he was doing and what he needed from her that he hadn't even thought about her reaction.

She was standing at the back of the warehouse, palms pressed against the rough boards, sobbing.

Jace stopped in front of her, unsure of what to say. "You knew him, didn't you?"

"I'm friends with his wife. They have two boys, Henry and Logan."

"I'm so sorry, Tess. I shouldn't have brought you out here like this. I wasn't thinking."

"He was always working hard for his family." She continued as if she hadn't heard his apology. "She told me sometimes he would come home after working security here at night and go straight to working their farm. She worried about him, but he cared so much about this community. Cared so much about seeing it thrive. Sofia taught me how to can tomatoes and make tortillas and tamales. She's the one that kept me coming back here. And now. . .she's just lost her world."

"I really am sorry."

"Who shot him?" she asked.

"I don't know, which is why I need your help."

"Can't you use your phone camera?"

"I can't rely on solar batteries and a phone that's constantly glitching. I could lose everything."

She wiped her cheeks with the back of her hand. "If I draw the sketches, will they help you find who did this to Jeremiah?"

Jace nodded. "That's what I'm hoping. You have such an eye for detail. I can't afford to miss anything."

"I'm not sure I'm good enough." Her hand trembled as she shoved a loose strand of hair behind her ear. "It's been so long since I've drawn anything."

He'd asked her once about her artwork, and she'd brushed him off. As far as he knew, she hadn't drawn anything since their mother died. Tess had always been hard to read and the one his parents had always worried about the most. The one he still worried about.

"You have a gift, Tess." Jace squeezed her hand. "Your work is emotional and moving. You see things other people don't see. I need you."

"Okay." She shoved her shoulders back.

"Are you sure?" he asked.

She nodded, then led the way back into the barn.

"This is going to help," Jace said. "I promise."

"I hope so."

"What about Frank?" Jace asked as they stepped back inside. "Did you know him?"

"I know he and Jeremiah were good friends. They were always laughing and cutting up. Sofia said it was to try to ease the tension."

Jace helped her pick up her art supplies. It was hard to find things to laugh about when every day was spent simply trying to survive.

"Where is Frank?" she asked.

"We don't know, but Tess—"

She bolted upright, her eyes wide with worry. "You think he could be dead too."

"We don't know." Jace squeezed her shoulder. "But thank you. What you're doing will help us find the truth."

She pulled out her sketchpad and a pencil. "People are going to panic when they realize Jeremiah was murdered."

"I know. That's why we've got to move quickly."

Tess had started on her second sketch when Levi returned to the warehouse.

"I spoke to Frank's wife," Levi said, crossing the cement floor to where Jace was. "He left for his shift just before dark last night, but she hasn't seen him since. She has no idea where he is."

"I'm going to have to talk with her." Jace let out a sharp breath. "And to Jeremiah's wife as well."

Of all the jobs he'd had to do over the past nine months, he hated this one the most. But this wasn't the first time he'd had to tell someone that their loved one was gone. And it wasn't the first time he'd had to tell someone that their spouse had been murdered.

CHAPTER SIX

JACE RODE BRISKET TO JEREMIAH DANIELS' home on the west side of town, a Spanish colonial built of solid-white brick and a clay-tiled roof. The piece of land it sat on was large and had a stunning view of the distant mountains. Jeremiah and Sofia had moved to Shadow Ridge over a decade ago and had quickly become a part of the community with their two children. And while he knew that the town would rally around her—especially those like Morgan who had also lost so much recently—this wasn't a road anyone wanted to walk down. And he hated the fact that he had to be the one to break the news to her.

Sofia stepped out onto the covered porch and wrapped her arms tightly around her waist as he made his way up the stairs. Her brown eyes darkened as if she knew this wasn't a social call.

"Sofia...I'm sorry to drop by unannounced," Jace started.

"What's happened? Because Jeremiah and I have told Henry if he gets in any more trouble—"

"It's not Henry." Jace paused, realizing his words were about to change this family's lives forever. "It's Jeremiah."

Sofia leaned against one of the porch posts. "What happened?"

Jace's heart pounded. "There's nothing I can say to soften the blow of what I need to tell you. Someone shot Jeremiah last night. I'm sorry, but. . .he's dead."

"No." Sofia stumbled backward. "You must be mistaken. He should be coming back from the warehouse any minute. He was working security there last night."

Jace grabbed Sofia's arm and walked her to the swing on the side of the porch, then sat down next to her. "He was. That's where we found him. I truly am sorry, Sofia."

She stared out across the porch, trying to absorb the news. News that her husband was never coming home again.

"Who did this?" she asked.

"We don't know. That's what we're trying to figure out—what we will figure out."

"What about Frank? He was there with him last night."

Jace hesitated again. "We don't know where Frank is. Levi's out trying to find him right now."

"Why would somebody kill him? All he wanted to do was support the town." Sofia looked up at him with tears in her eyes. "I always told him that guarding all that food was dangerous. That one day he wasn't going to come home."

"I'm so sorry."

She shook her head. "What am I going to do? How am I supposed to take care of our sons and make sure they have enough to eat? I can't do this on my own."

"You're not going to be alone, Sofia." Jace grasp her hand. "I can't imagine how hard this is, but you've seen the town rally in support this past year. We're in this together. We'll make sure you're okay."

"The town, their support. . .none of that can take the place of my husband."

Jace searched for the right thing to say to her. Something

that would fix the situation. But he knew that nothing he said or did could make Jeremiah come back. Nothing could put back together this woman's shattered world.

Footsteps on the porch shifted his attention. Frank's wife, Judith, stepped onto the porch, her colorful skirt blowing in the wind.

"Sofia, what's wrong?"

"Jeremiah's dead," Sofia said, her voice void of emotion.

"What?" Judith looked at Jace. "Levi told me Frank was missing, but nothing about Jeremiah. I don't understand. What happened?"

"We don't know yet, but I promise. . .we will find out." Jace got up off the swing as Judith pulled Sofia into her arms. "I know this is difficult, but I'm going to need to ask you some questions, Judith. In private, as soon as I can."

"No." Judith shook her head. "Sofia is my best friend. Anything you need to say, you can say it in front of her."

"Go ahead, please," Sofia said. "Jeremiah might be gone, but we need to find Frank."

Jace nodded. "When's the last time you saw Frank?"

"Like I told your brother, he left after dinner last night for the warehouse like he does every time it's his shift. Both of them did, actually. Jeremiah stopped by and they left together."

Jace thought about what he needed to know from Judith without implying that Frank might be guilty. He knew that the two men had been friends for years, and he'd never seen any indication of trouble between the two of them. But still, a lot had changed in the past few months.

"Have you noticed anything different about Frank recently?"

"Different? How am I supposed to answer that?" Judith's voice rose as she spoke. "Everyone is different. Nothing is normal for anyone anymore. A year ago, my oldest son had letters of acceptance to five major universities. Now I have to bribe him to work in the garden and then send him around trying to trade things. My two youngest were ecstatic about a vacation we were planning to take to Disneyworld this summer. Now we don't know if we will ever get to go, and there certainly isn't going to be a fairy-tale ending to all of this."

Jace drew in a deep breath, hating the pain he was causing with his questions.

"And as for Frank," she continued, "he spends all his time just trying to keep our family together, and in his spare time he helps make sure the town stays secure. So whatever you're thinking, Frank didn't do. He's a good man, who loves God, his community, and his family."

He fought to hold the woman's gaze. "So there were no issues between the two men?"

"If you're implying that Frank and Jeremiah got in a fight that ended with him shooting Jeremiah?" Sofia broke in. "You're way off base."

"I'm not trying to imply anything, but I am worried about your husband," Jace said, struggling to get the answers he needed without digging himself into an even deeper hole.

There was no way to check the blood they'd found for DNA or dust for fingerprints, which was why the questions he was asking were essential. They knew that Frank was worried about having enough food and that there were plenty of places to sell stolen goods. The bottom line was that people forced into a corner often did things they normally would never do.

"I know these are hard questions," he started again, "which is why if there's anything you know that might help us find him —anything at all—I need to know."

Judith leaned forward, her mouth pulled into a grim line.

"Frank struggled to keep food on the table for our family, but nothing would get him to stoop low enough to go against what he believes is right and wrong. You know my husband and have seen how hard he's worked for this town."

"Yes, I have."

"Then go out and find him, instead of accusing him of something we both know he didn't do."

"I know what kind of man Frank is, and I don't think that he is behind this. But in order to find the truth, I have to make sure we don't miss anything that might help." Jace cleared his throat. "Can I have your permission to search your property?"

"What are you looking for?"

Jace hesitated with his answer. "Honestly, I don't know."

"I don't care. We have nothing to hide." Judith's usual friendly expression was guarded. "But I'd like to stay with Sofia. Gideon's there if you need anything. He was there when Levi stopped by, and knows his father is missing, but his younger brothers. . .I don't want them to know."

"Of course. I'll keep you updated."

Jace headed back down the porch stairs while the two women whispered to each other. Blue skies hovered above him as he started toward Frank's adjoining property that was set on a couple of acres of land. A dog barked in the distance. Birds chirped atop useless power lines. Gardens had popped up in people's yards as they worked to plant enough food to get through the winter. Those who lived on bigger plots of land outside town now took to the surrounding acres of land to hunt for meat and fish. Empty houses, vacant of the lives and laughter that once filled them, were on every block, making parts of Shadow Ridge feel more like one of the forgotten towns he used to explore with his parents and siblings.

He headed first to the barn that sat east of the stone and

stucco house, unable to ignore the truth in Judith's testimony. Frank had always been an outstanding member of the community and had been one of the first ones to step up, willing to do anything needed as they organized and figured out the new normal. But the man did have a temper. Jace had seen it more than once. Stress had become a constant companion to many—fear of what was out there, fear of the unknown, and fear of what they would face tomorrow.

And sometimes that fear made a person lose perspective.

Jace tried to shake his own nagging fears. The last time he had been here Frank had showed him his new pet project, raising pigs. They must be doing well because the stench from the A-frame shed and fenced mud pit behind the barn filled his nostrils. Keeping livestock meant both food and a source of fertilizers for the gardens, all of which had become essential.

He stepped inside the barn and squinted at the typical setup with animal stalls on either side and a hayloft above. Everything was neat and tidy. From the tools hanging on the wall to the unusable mower and leaf blower in the corner. A couple of the animal stalls held the Savages' two mares, now more valuable than a vehicle.

Jace walked down the middle of the barn, stopping at each stall as he went. In the last stall, a tarp had been stuffed behind a pile of hay bales. He maneuvered his way toward the wall, then pulled the worn tarp back. Beneath it lay four grain bags he was sure had come from the warehouse. Which in itself wasn't unusual, they gave out the bags to families, but the limit was two per family.

He moved a couple of them aside and discovered something else was hidden beneath them. An empty box of military explosives. Jace took a step backward, trying to make sense of what he was looking at. Frank had been a chemistry teacher in the local schools. But explosives? What did he need them for? Typically, explosives were traced in order to track their movement and aid in identifying suspects connected to criminal activity, but that wasn't going to be possible.

Something else caught his eye. A blood stain on the side of the box.

We can't ignore the possibility that this might have been an inside job.

Jace had brushed off his brother's statement. The thought that Frank actually might've betrayed the town left a sour feeling in his stomach. He turned back toward the door, still not ready to jump to conclusions. Somewhere in all of this there had to be an explanation because the evidence he'd found was far from conclusive.

He started to walk back outside, then stopped. An old tobacco tin had been stuffed behind the door. He opened it up and sniffed. It was the same mixture as he'd found in the warehouse.

The large barn door creaked open, and he stepped back out of the way, still holding the tin.

"Gideon."

Frank and Judith's oldest had just turned eighteen, and from a couple talks with Frank, and the confirmation earlier today from his mother, Jace knew the young man was struggling. It was hard to blame him. The Quake had changed everything he knew in the blink of an eye, and had taken with it all his dreams for his future.

"Officer McQuaid. I thought I heard someone out here."

"I was actually just coming to find you. I spoke to your mother. She said I could look around."

Gideon shoved his hands into his pockets. "I was here when your brother came earlier. He said my father is missing."

"Yes, but we're going to find him. I'm just looking around,

seeing if anything might explain where he might have gone." Jace held up the tobacco tin. "Gideon, did your father use this?"

"No. He didn't smoke."

"Do you know why it's here?"

The young man stared at the ground, avoiding his gaze.

"Gideon. . ."

"It's mine."

"Where did you get it?"

"A guy sold it to me."

"Where?"

Gideon shrugged.

Jace decided to try another approach. "I need to know where you got this, Gideon. It could be connected to your father's disappearance."

"Fine. Behind the school."

"Do you know the name of the seller?"

"No." The defensiveness was back in Gideon's voice. "But it's not like it's a crime."

"How old are you?"

"Eighteen."

"I assume you know that the law prohibits anyone under twenty-one to possess, purchase, or consume tobacco products."

"What are you going to do?" Gideon let out a low laugh. "The whole world is falling apart. I can't see how an underage tobacco law really matters at this point."

"It matters to me, and I'm pretty sure it matters to your parents as well," Jace said. "Not to mention the person who broke the law by selling it to you."

"I thought being a cop meant you knew what was going on around here, so you could keep us safe, but I guess I was wrong."

"I know that a bunch of the high school kids play cards and

gamble for alcohol shots inside the empty theater. I know Old Crosby sells cigarettes and moonshine to anyone who will pay, including minors, and that Crosby also waters down his moonshine so he can make more. And yes, those things still matter and are being dealt with."

Gideon dropped his gaze. "Fine. You made your point."

"Do you know where your father might go if he was in trouble?"

"You think he did something?"

"I don't know. Right now, I just want to find him."

The anger in Gideon's gaze had turned to fear. "The only thing I can think of is he has a secret fishing hole he goes to when he's stressed. I followed him out there one day. I don't think anyone but me and him knows where it is."

"Where is it?"

"There's an old boat ramp on the east side of the reservoir near Michael Granary's land. You can find bass, crappie, and catfish on a good day."

And hopefully your father.

"Thank you." Jace pocketed the tobacco tin, then headed out the door. "But don't think you're getting off for this. We'll talk about it later with your parents."

"Whatever." Gideon ran to catch up with him. "Where are you going?"

"To put together a search party to find your father."

"I'm coming with you. I've got a horse, and I can ride."

Jace stopped and turned around. "I'm not sure your mother would want—"

"If my father's missing and needs help, I'm coming with you."

Jace started to say no, then changed his mind. It might be best to keep the boy nearby and out of trouble.

"I'll let you come on two conditions," Jace said.

"Fine."

"Your mother's next door at the Daniels. If she gives her permission for you to join us, you can meet me at the police station. But if you do come with me, you'll do exactly what I tell you."

CHAPTER SEVEN

IT WAS the third search party Jace had organized in the last month, with the town's solar sirens signaling each time the need for volunteers. Three weeks ago, Carrie Hernandez's three-year-old son had wondered off from her front porch. They'd found him four hours later, scared, but safe. Then last week, they'd organized another search for a man with Alzheimer's who'd decided he needed to hitchhike to Dallas to see his son. They'd found him on the highway on the edge of town, waiting for a passing car. And now they were searching for Frank, unsure if he was a victim or a murder suspect.

They'd discovered early on that searching without radios enabling them to communicate with a central command post amplified the difficulty of finding a missing person. To better facilitate a ground search, Jace had put into place a system where each volunteer had a ready-packed bag with essentials like maps, first-aid supplies, a knife, and matches so they were ready to go as soon as the town sirens went off. Today, twelve volunteers had split up in pairs, each assigned to a specific grid on the map. Once each team completed their area, they were to meet back at an established base. If the person was found, a single flare was shot into the air.

Another obstacle that made a search challenging was the unique landscape. While the town of Shadow Ridge was surrounded by ranch land and pecan and apple orchards, there were also prairies and canyons, and not far beyond the arid terrain was an expanse of cooler, forested mountains.

FRANK'S last known position was either the warehouse where he'd worked last night, or his property where they'd found traces of blood in his barn. With no way to narrow the search perimeters, he and Gideon had started at the fishing hole, but there had been no sign of anyone being there recently.

At the moment, riding with Gideon, Jace felt as if they were searching blind without any real clues. In a typical search, you could minimize the area by having a starting point and time and then determining how fast the person is traveling. But with limited manpower and no way to know which direction the man had gone, every minute that passed lessened the odds of finding him before dark.

Jace glanced over at Gideon as they headed back through the trees. He'd been impressed with the boy's attitude once they'd hit the trail. While he hadn't said much, he also hadn't complained as he kept his focus on the search. But he had to be growing frustrated. Three hours into their search and there was still no sign of his father. Instead, all they'd seen were miles and miles of grasslands, scattered bushes, and trees along with an occasional mule deer or small herds of sheep.

"How are you doing?" Jace handed him a thick piece of beef jerky out of his bag. "I know this is tough on you."

Gideon hesitated, then took it.

"My father and I have had a lot of ups and downs in our

relationship," Jace said, when Gideon didn't answer. "Especially when I was your age. And I also know the added stress of the last year has changed everything."

"I was supposed to leave this place six months ago, but now. . .now I'm stuck."

"I understand more than you think. I was back for my parents' anniversary. I never planned to stay."

That piece of information seemed to click in Gideon's mind. "You're in the military, aren't you?"

"I was. I got out right before coming here. And believe it or not, you're the first person I've told," Jace said, surprised with his own confession.

"What were you planning to do?"

Jace let out a low chuckle. "Anything but law enforcement."

"That's ironic, considering you're now the law around here."

"Very ironic, though I've learned over the years that life has a way of throwing the unexpected at you and you have to be flexible enough to go with the punches."

"Why did you want to leave the military?"

Jace tugged gently on the reins, keeping Brisket heading to the left as the trail forked. The question dug into a place he wasn't sure he wanted to go. Even his family didn't know the details of what had happened on his last assignment. But they were the same details that haunted his dreams at night.

"There was an accident where a lot of people died," he said finally. "And I. . .I blame myself."

"Was it really your fault?"

"I guess." Jace hesitated. "I'll never know what would have happened if I'd done things differently."

They rode on in silence a few more minutes, still searching for signs of Frank. But the desert seemed to only whisper back to them an eerie silence.

"My father doesn't understand," Gideon said finally. "Like

my mom, he thinks it's wonderful we're all together. Or at least that's what he wants me to think. But I was supposed to be away at school. Instead, I'm stuck in a place I always wanted to get away from."

"I bet he understands more than you think," Jace said. "He's had a lot to carry the last few months. Not only has he worked to keep your family together, but the town as well. It's been a lot of responsibility and stress."

They started up a slight ridge with trees on one side, rocky outcrops on the other, and forested mountains in the distance. "I guess I never thought about it that way, but yeah."

"What were you planning to study?"

"I wanted to be an engineer, but there's no way I will now. I'll be spending the rest of my life watching my brothers, making sure the garden stays weeded, and caring for those stinky ol' pigs."

"We don't know if that's true, but those are pretty important jobs at the moment."

Gideon's frown deepened. "I know. My father keeps reminding me."

"I know this is hard." Jace searched for what to say. "But I also know that sometimes the small things we do are just as important as the big things we do."

"Yeah. I just. . .I feel so trapped."

Jace tightened his grip on the reins. Looking at Gideon was like looking in the mirror. He'd come back to Shadow Ridge, not out of a sense of duty, but because he was lost and needed answers. And he'd never told anyone.

"He didn't do it," Gideon said. "My father. No matter how mad I get at him, I know he would never hurt anyone."

"I believe you."

"And if I never see him again? Then what?"

Jace took in a long, deep breath of the familiar musky and

earthy smells. "I've had a lot of regrets in my life. My father and I are close, but we haven't always been that way. And now, taking over his job here in Shadow Ridge, there've been a lot of days when I wanted to walk away."

"You didn't have to take the job."

"No, but sometimes a man has to stand up for what's right, even when he doesn't think he has the strength to do it. Good men like your father, and Jeremiah."

"And when you don't know how?" Gideon asked.

It was an honest question. A question he'd asked more than he cared to admit. "I don't have all the answers by any means, but I do know that's where faith comes in. Standing firm, being courageous, and finding strength in a steadfast God."

"That's not easy."

"No," Jace said. "No, it's not."

A flare went off on the ridge to their south.

Gideon's face went ashen as red streaked across the skyline. "They found my father."

Ten minutes later, Gideon jumped off his horse ahead of Jace and ran to where three of the teams were already gathered on the bank ten feet above a slow-moving creek. "Where's my father?"

"Hold on." Levi held up his hands. "We have a problem. Frank—"

"Don't tell me he's dead," Gideon begged. "Please. . . He can't be dead."

Jace wrapped his arm around the boy's shoulders, afraid his decision to allow Gideon to come with them had been a mistake. "Let Levi talk, Gideon. We'll face whatever's going on together."

"Your father's not dead." Levi hesitated.

"Then where is he?" Gideon asked.

"Frank's the one who set off the flare. He's on the other side of the creek." Levi motioned to the opposite ridge. "Keaton Howell is with him, and. . .and Frank's holding him hostage."

Jace shifted his attention to the opposite bank, then blew out a sharp breath of frustration. Frank was standing over Keaton, who was blindfolded, and holding a gun to his head. "So he was what. . .tracking our teams?"

"It looks that way."

"No. . ." Gideon tried to run toward the narrow trail that led down to the creek, but Jace pulled him back.

"I need you to stay here with me, Gideon. At least until we know what's going on."

"You don't understand. My father would never do something like this."

"How did this happen?" Jace asked Levi. "How did he get Keaton?"

"I don't know. Keaton heard something, and went to see what it was. The next thing I know, the flare was going off. I thought he'd located Frank, but when I got here this is what I found."

"Jace McQuaid?" Frank yelled from the other side of the bank. "I've been waiting for you."

Jace turned to Gideon. "I'm going to talk with your dad, but I need you to promise me you'll stay here with Levi."

Gideon stared across the gully where his father stood on the other side.

"Gideon?" Jace prodded.

The boy nodded.

Jace stepped up to the edge of the bank where water trickled down through the rocky creek bed below. "It's me, Frank. I don't know what's going on, but I need you to put the gun down and let Keaton go. I want to end this before someone else gets hurt, and I think you do to."

Frank shook his head. "Sorry, I can't do that."

"I know you've been struggling Frank, but I can help."

"That's where you're wrong. You've done everything you can to fix this town, but you can't fix this. You can't bring Jeremiah back."

"Do you know what happened to Jeremiah?" Jace asked.

"That's not why I'm here."

"Then why are we here, Frank? I know Jeremiah was your friend. And your wife... She doesn't know what happened to you." Jace prayed for the words that would convince Frank to put an end to this. "Frank, your son is here. You don't want him to see this. I've always known you to be an upstanding man. I know things are hard, but this isn't going to help anything. Let Keaton go, and we'll figure this out."

"It's too late for that."

"No it's not. Frank, I know you're scared. I know you don't see a way."

Jace took a step back, needing to reevaluate his approach. Listening was important in any kind of negotiation. But when even the thought of his own son seeing this play out didn't soften the man's heart, Jace wasn't sure what would.

"Then tell me what you want," Jace said, resting his hands on his hips. "Tell me why we're here. I promise I'll listen."

"I need weapons, food, and horses."

Despite the demand, Jace could hear the fear in his voice. There had to be a way to talk him off the ledge.

"Where are you planning to go, Frank?" Jace asked. "You know it's not safe out there. This desert is filled with bandits and troublemakers."

"That's not your problem. I want all of you to take your weapons and any food you have and load them onto two of the horses. Then one of you take them up fifty yards downstream to the clearing and tie them to a tree."

"I need you to give me a minute—"

"Do you think this is all a joke?" Frank's voice rose. "You've got five minutes or Keaton is dead."

Dead.

A switch in Jace's mind flipped.

Wind whipped around him. Dark clouds gathered, pressing down the heat around him. But this was a different desert. There had been six of them in the Hummer that day. Six of them who were in the wrong place at the wrong time. Pauly was the group's chaplain. The one who made them laugh. The one who gave them good advice about their girlfriends back home. He'd quote Scripture to them and remind them that there was going to be life after all of this. Sand blew around Jace, the hot grit that seemed to find its way into every crevice of his body. But that's not what he was thinking about. Not with the man holding Pauly with a gun to his head.

Jace heard the crack of a pistol, snapping his attention back to Frank and Keaton.

"Jace? Jace, can you hear me?"

His head throbbed. Temples pulsing. He shook his head and looked across the valley. The flowing robes of the gunmen vanished and were replaced with Frank's jeans and flannel shirt.

Jace squeezed his eyes shut. He needed to focus. To stay in the present. But flashbacks had become all too real as one trauma triggered another. The marks of PTSD gouging into his consciousness weren't just in the nightmares that came while he slept. But he couldn't allow any distractions today. Couldn't lose this round. He'd spent the past two years interrogating prisoners. Two years gathering information, convincing people to give him the answers he needed. Now he wasn't sure he would have the skills to successfully avert a crisis that could end another life.

"Jace."

He opened his eyes. Levi stood in front of him, waiting for him to give directions.

"Jace. . . What do you want us to do?"

"We do what he said," Jace said, taking control of himself once again. "Whatever his plan is, he won't get far. And this time we'll make sure he doesn't take any more hostages."

"Wait a minute. . ." Gideon ran up to the edge and shouted across the ravine. "Why are you doing this, Dad?"

"Gideon—" Jace started after Gideon.

"I'm doing this for you. Get my son out of here."

Jace grasped Gideon's shoulder, holding him back.

"Why would he do this?"

"There comes a time when you feel so trapped you don't know which way is up," Jace said. "You almost forget how to breathe."

He knew because he'd been there.

Jace heard the explosion a second before he saw the thick plume of black smoke on the horizon, coming from the direction of Shadow Ridge. He started shouting out orders, because even though he was no expert, he knew from the height of the smoke and the volume of the blast that they were looking at some kind of powerful explosive.

Like from the box he'd found in Frank's barn.

CHAPTER EIGHT

MORGAN FELT the ground shake beneath her the second the blast wave hit. Unprepared for the impact, she stumbled forward, scraping her knee against the sidewalk. Glass shattered behind her. Someone screamed. Her lungs filled with smoke. Rubble fell from the crumbling façade of what once was the bank, while a tornado of flying debris swirled around her.

She choked on the dust as she stumbled to her feet, trying to avoid the glass. Trying to make sense of the chaos. While Shadow Ridge sometimes felt more like an abandoned town with dozens of businesses closed, a few buildings on Main Street, like the library, had become a place for people to connect. But now, the bank was nothing more than a pile of debris, framed by shattered store windows on either side of the building.

Morgan searched the smoke for the injured and found Claire West sitting on the sidewalk a few feet in front of her, looking dazed. Morgan headed toward the college student as a small crowd began to form.

"Claire. . . Claire are you okay?" Blood ran down the girl's face from a gash on her head.

"I don't know." Claire's hand trembled as she wiped her cheek. "I was heading to the library when. . .I don't even know what happened."

"Can you remember anything?" Morgan asked, quickly ripping off the button- down shirt she was wearing over a tank top. She pulled back Claire's hair, then pressed the fabric against the gash.

"I was planning to meet Nora. She was going to help me with some dress patterns. And then. . .the next thing I remember was a thunderous explosion, and I was on my back."

"There's a cut on your head," Morgan said. "Probably from flying debris. I don't think it's that bad, but you might need stiches. Hope's going to need to check it out. Do you think you can get up?"

"I think so."

"Morgan. . ." Sadie Mae, who used to be a regular at the diner, squatted down next to her. "Are the two of you okay?"

Morgan nodded. "She's got a gash on her head. I need to get her to the clinic."

"Alec Miller and his daughter have similar injuries. We'll make sure no one else was injured, then be right behind you with them."

Morgan choked on the smoke that filled the air as she helped Claire to her feet, put her arm around the young woman's waist, then headed down the street toward the clinic. The surrounding chaos was a reminder of just how quickly things could spiral out of control. But an explosion at the bank didn't make sense. Cash wasn't worth the paper it was printed on.

A flash of red caught Morgan's attention, distracting her for a moment. She watched as a man wearing a ball cap made his way around the crowd—heading away from those gathered close to the edges of the explosion radius. His gait and the way he carried himself triggered memories. . .

Ricky?

She hesitated, trying to get another look at him as he disappeared behind the crowd, but lost him. No. She shifted her attention back to Claire. It couldn't be Ricky. The last time she'd seen her brother-in-law, he'd come through Shadow Ridge with another one of his stories, asking for money before heading out of town again. He'd told Tommy he was heading to Washington State, where he'd been hired to work on a commercial fishing boat. That was over a year ago.

Claire stumbled next to her as they continued down Main Street toward the clinic.

"Are you feeling dizzy?" Morgan asked, tightening her grip around Claire's waist.

"A little."

"Hang on. We're almost there."

Morgan stepped into the clinic for the second time that day. "Hope?"

Hope rushed into the lobby, carrying her first responder kit. "Morgan. I was about to head out and see what had happened."

"There was an explosion at the bank. Claire was hit on the head with some flying debris. From what I can tell, most of the blood is from a gash on her head, but she's also got some cuts on her arms and legs."

"What about you?" Hope asked. "You're bleeding."

Morgan looked down and saw the trails of blood on her arm for the first time. "It's nothing. I'm fine."

"I'll check you next. Was anyone else hurt?" Hope led them to a room with four beds with curtain dividers.

"Sadie Mae's coming behind me with at least two others who were hit by debris."

"Where's Noah?"

"He's safe. It's his afternoon to play with Mateo, and I wanted to keep things as normal as possible for him." Morgan paused, not missing the irony in her words. There was nothing normal about today. Nothing normal about anything. "What can I do? I had first-aid training back in college."

"With both my nurses out, you're hired," Hope said, pulling out the supplies they were going to need. "Except for the gash on Claire's head, it looks like most of these cuts are superficial, but there are quite a few on her leg. If you'll put on some gloves and clean them with soap and water, I'll look at her head." Hope turned to Claire. "What's the last thing you remember?"

Morgan felt herself move into auto pilot—something she'd done far too much this past year simply in order to survive—as Hope started asking Claire a string of questions. There were more days than she wanted to count when her mind and body wanted to run away from all of this and she had to fight against completely shutting down. But then Noah would come up to her with his big brown eyes and his daddy's smile, and she'd remember she wasn't just doing this for herself. Noah had already lost a father. He couldn't lose his mother too.

Today she refused to sink into that familiar dark hole as Sadie Mae brought Alec and his nine-year-old daughter into the clinic. Hope signaled for Morgan to look at the daughter while she examined the father.

Morgan lifted the girl up onto the exam table. "Your name's Grace, right?"

The girl nodded.

"This might sting," Morgan said, thankful that all she saw were a couple of scrapes. "I'm just going to clean these up so they won't get infected, and then as soon as the doctor sees you, you should be able to go home."

The girl wrinkled her nose and poked at her ears. "I can't hear very well."

"The blast was loud, wasn't it?" Morgan said.

Grace nodded again.

"I'll make sure the doctor looks at your ears, but mine are ringing too. It should go away."

"Is my daddy going to be okay?"

Is my daddy going to be okay?

Noah had asked the same question the day Tommy had died. There had been no easy answer then, but today. . .Morgan let out a sharp breath of air. No. She wasn't going to let herself go back there.

"Dr. McQuaid is taking care of your daddy right now, and trust me. . ." Morgan smiled at Grace as she cleaned the last cut. "She's a really good doctor."

"I know." Grace winced, as Morgan put some ointment on the cut.

"Sorry."

"It's okay," Grace said, squeezing her eyes shut for a moment. "Dr. Hope made me a cast when I broke my arm, but it hurt a whole lot more than this."

Morgan laughed. "Well, you're very brave."

"Hey, ladybug." Grace's dad walked over to them. "Are you okay?"

"Yes, but my ears won't stop ringing."

Hope quickly looked Grace over, then took a step back and set her hands on her hips. "If they're still ringing in a couple of days, come back and see me, but the two of you are good to go."

Hope helped her hop down from the exam table, then Grace wrapped her arms around her father.

"Thank you," Alec said. "Both of you."

"This could have been a whole lot worse," Morgan said as the bell above the door rang and the pair walked out.

"I know, but thankfully everyone should be fine, though I am going to keep Claire for observation a little bit longer." Hope stepped in front of Morgan. "And I need to look at your arm. There's one above your elbow that might need a couple stitches."

"Let me clean up a bit first," Morgan said.

She went to one of the plastic pitchers of water, grabbed a cloth, and tried to scrub the blood off her white tank top. But instead of coming off, the red stain continued to spread across the fabric. Panic bubbled as she rubbed harder.

"Morgan?"

She jumped at Hope's hand on her arm.

"Are you okay?"

"I can't get the stain out," Morgan said. "It just keeps spreading."

Hope clasped her hands, pulling her fingers away from the fabric. "Hey. The only thing that matters is that you're okay. I've got some hydrogen peroxide that will help get that out."

Suddenly, she was crying, all over a stupid shirt. Except she knew her tears had nothing to do with a stain.

Morgan stepped back from the water, dried her hands, then dropped them to her sides. "How do you get the images out of your head?"

"Tommy?"

Morgan closed her eyes for a moment. Hope had been there. On the afternoon of the Quake, a semi had gone through the only stoplight in town, T-boning Tommy's car and then hitting Hope's mother. Both had died instantly.

"I know you understand," Morgan said finally. "Your mother died in the same wreck, but sometimes. . .sometimes I just can't shake the images. And then something like today triggers it all over again."

Hope squeezed her hands. "Let me clean you up."

Morgan worked to slow her breathing as Hope started cleaning the scratches on her arm.

"Tell me what you're feeling," Hope said.

"I don't know what's going on." Morgan shook her head, then grabbed a tissue from the box and blew her nose. "The men are out searching for Frank. Jeremiah is dead. . .murdered. My son saw his dead body, and now this. . .this explosion. I just feel. . .numb."

"That's understandable," Hope said, catching her gaze. "You're carrying a lot."

"And I'm terrified of losing someone else. Worried about what kind of world this is going to be for Noah. He's already lost his father. There are so many *what ifs* that if it weren't for him, I'm not sure I'd have the energy to get up most mornings."

Hope pulled up a stool and sat down in front of her. "As a doctor, my first instinct is to want to fix all of this, but this past year has shown me I can't. All I can do is keep my eyes fixed on God and remember that all of this is temporary. And remind you of the same thing."

Morgan felt her thoughts swirl. But was it temporary? Even if the grid came back on and they managed to find some sense of normalcy again, Tommy was never coming back.

"At least you can hang on to the hope that Chase will return." Morgan felt the sting of her harsh words the moment they came out. She pressed her hand against her mouth and shook her head. "I'm sorry. I shouldn't have said that. I just—"

"Forget it." Hope squeezed her hand. "Seriously. Today—if possible—has been even more unsettling than normal, between having to deal with Noah, then Jeremiah, and now this. Besides, what are best friends for if they can't vent to each other. You know you can always come to me to talk and say anything you need to."

"I know, but there's something else," Morgan said, wishing

Hope's reassurance would help stem the flow of guilt for both her calloused words and her lack of faith. "I think I saw Tommy's brother in the crowd after the explosion."

"Ricky?"

Morgan nodded.

"You need to tell Jace."

"But Ricky was supposed to be up in the Pacific northwest when all of this happened. There's no way he could be here. I had to have imagined it."

"And if you didn't imagine it?"

"Jace needs to know, but if I'm wrong, I'd just be sending him off on a wild goose chase."

Compounded stress and fatigue pressed against her chest. She just couldn't be a hundred percent certain that the man she'd seen was Ricky. And even if he was here, she had no proof he was involved in the explosion. On the other hand, she knew Ricky well enough to know that if he was here, he wasn't up to anything good.

Hope caught Morgan's gaze. "What's going on between you and Jace?"

"Me and Jace?" Morgan tried to keep the tremor out of her voice at the question. "Nothing. Why?"

She'd never admitted to Hope or really even to herself for that matter, her conflicting feelings toward him. What bothered her was that she couldn't deny that she looked forward to his visits and the chance to spend time with him. Which was why she'd come up with a dozen excuses why she shouldn't go talk to Jace—even about Ricky.

Because she'd seen the way he looked at her. His eyes lingering a few seconds too long. He always said he was just doing his job, but she knew it was more than that. She's noted too many chance encounters and excuses for him to stop by. And right now, she wasn't sure what she was most worried about. That Ricky was back in town, that Jace might be falling in love with her, or that she was starting to feel something toward him.

Morgan glanced down at her wedding ring. A part of her wished she could take it off. Wished that she could eventually move on with someone else. But her heart wasn't ready, and as hard as it was to face each day on her own, loneliness wasn't a reason to give it away. Noah deserved better than that. She deserved better than that.

But if all of that was true, then why couldn't she stop thinking about him?

No. Morgan forced herself to gain control of her thoughts. What she felt or didn't feel toward Jace McQuaid didn't matter right now. What mattered was that they find whoever did this, and if Ricky was possibly involved, Jace needed to know.

CHAPTER NINE

JACE QUESTIONED his decision to leave Levi to deal with Frank the entire ride back to Shadow Ridge. Not that his brother wasn't capable of handling the situation. He'd finished the required thirty-six weeks of training and had started his field training just before the grid had gone down. But he still lacked experience. And now, without the luxury of being able to call for backup from the county sheriff, or any branch of law enforcement for that matter, they were going in on their own.

Jace could smell the heavy scent of smoke in the air as he rode into Shadow Ridge and headed down Main Street with Max and Hernandez. He'd sent someone to take Gideon home, convincing the boy that his mother needed him right now, but he worried about how Gideon was going to deal with what he'd seen.

A minute later the target of the explosion came into view. It looked as if most of the damage was in the back of the building, but the entire face of the bank had crumbled into a pile of bricks, leaving sunlight to filter through the roof where there were now large gaps in the tile. A crowd had formed around the front, trying to figure out—like he was—exactly what was going on.

"Max," Jace said, barking orders. "Start interviewing as many people as you can. I want to talk to anyone who saw something."

The empty box of dynamite he'd found inside Frank's barn couldn't be a coincidence, but they needed to know how it was connected and who else was behind this.

"Hernandez, there's crime scene tape at the police station," Jace continued. "First cabinet, bottom drawer on the right. We need this area cordoned off ASAP."

"I'm on it."

"I need everyone back." Jace waved at several bystanders, worried about the aftereffects of the structural damage, but also the possibility of a second explosion.

"I was here when it went off." Aaron Knight, former owner of the hardware store, stepped up to him. "Whoever is behind this must have known what they were doing. No one was in the bank, obviously, and the blast seems to have been contained there."

"Was anyone hurt?" Jace asked.

"From what I saw several were hit by flying debris and were taken immediately to the clinic."

"I need you to get me an update on the injuries," Jace said.

"Of course. I'll be back."

A moment later, Jace stepped into what was left of the bank. The smell of acid and smoke filled his nostrils. Charred remains of lobby furniture sat next to piles of bricks that had fallen during the explosion. Of all the things that he'd feared during the last year, this had not been one of them. Why rob a bank when money was worthless? He walked up to the once-secure bank vault then crouched down next to a couple wires peeking out from in the rubble.

He pulled a pad of paper out of his back pocket and made a couple of rudimentary sketches of the scene that included an inventory of what had been exposed.

Hernandez stepped up behind him. "I have the tape up. Aaron returned from the clinic and said there were several with cuts and scrapes, but no serious injuries."

"That's good news. Do you know who?"

"Claire West, Alec Miller and his daughter Grace, and Morgan."

Morgan?

Jace tried to push away the panic at her name, along with the numerous questions that followed. "And you're sure there were no serious injuries?"

"That's what your sister said."

"Ok." Jace nodded. He'd have to worry about following up on Morgan later. "Thank you."

"Aaron will make sure the crowd stays back," Hernandez continued. "I also told him to let us know if the bank manager shows up."

"Good. I appreciate it."

"What do you think they were after?" Hernandez asked.

"I don't know." Jace continued working on his rough sketch of the charred remains and twisted metal, wishing Tess were here. "It looks to me like dynamite was the source of the explosion. It ripped through the back of the bank, hitting both the money vault and the safety deposit room and damaging the lobby."

"I can understand the need to rob our food storage and the clinic, but a bank vault? It doesn't make sense."

"I've been wondering the same thing, but there's the safety deposit boxes," Jace said, adding a few notes. "Maybe there was something inside one of them that somebody wanted."

"If that's true, they went to a lot of trouble for whatever was inside." Hernandez stepped over a pile of cement. "Especially when most of what's in there is probably worthless."

Jace frowned. Paperwork, property deeds, jewelry, other personal items—most had no real value anymore. A coin machine had somehow survived the blast along with bags of untouched coins still needing to be processed. A year ago, he could see why somebody might want to do this. But today? Today those coins were as worthless as his dead cell phone.

"Jace. . ." Hernandez said. "Look at this."

Jace made his way over to the corner of the bank vault. "What is it?"

Hernandez squatted next to a small trunk. "This was buried behind the fallen wall. It's full of emergency supplies. Looks like non-perishable food, a first-aid kit, some prescription medication, a hand-cranked radio, water treatment tablets. . ."

"All worth more than their weight in gold." Something shiny caught Jace's gaze, and he bent over and picked up a silver coin. "This is odd. It must have come from one of the safe deposit boxes."

He handed it to Hernandez, who held it up to the light. "It's a Buffalo nickel. My father used to collect these."

Hernandez handed it back to him.

"Jace?" Aaron's silhouette appeared in the doorway. "The bank manager's here."

"Good," Jace said, slipping the coin into his pocket. "Will you please escort him to the police station, Aaron? I'll be there in a few minutes. And Hernandez, have Max help you keep the scene secure."

Jace took a couple additional minutes to finish his sketches and notes on the scene, needing them to be as thorough as possible before the sun began to set, then headed back out of the rubble to where Owen Waybright, the bank manager, and Aaron were waiting for him just outside the police station.

"None of you have any right to keep me off the bank property," Owen said as soon as Jace had crossed the street.

Jace held up his hand. "You'll be able to go in later, but in case you didn't notice, the bank is now an active crime scene."

Owen frowned. "I did notice. Who in the world would want to blow up a bank?"

"That's what I'm trying to find out," Jace said, signaling for him to follow inside so their conversation wouldn't be overheard. "I'm going to need to ask you some questions."

"You don't understand." Owen jabbed his finger toward the bank. "I need to get inside there. I've got to go through everything and make sure my clients' safe security boxes aren't tampered with, plus somehow find another location—"

"I'll make sure the place is guarded until it's safe to go inside," Jace interrupted, pointing to a chair. "But if we're going to figure out who did this, I'm going to need some answers."

"Except I don't have any answers. I have no idea why somebody would do this."

"Who had access to the vault and its contents?" Jace leaned back against the desk.

"Me and Lois, one of the tellers."

"Do you know why there would be a trunk of emergency supplies in your bank vault?"

Owen shrugged. "No, but I'm not the one who normally checks things in and out of the vault. That would be Lois."

"I saw her outside the bank," Aaron said. "I can go get her."

Jace nodded his thanks, then turned back to Owen. He needed to find a way to diffuse the man's defensiveness. While the piles of coins and even paper money had no value anymore, black-market trading had become a big business, and there could easily have been more boxes stored inside the vault. It was the perfect hiding place, where no one would ever think to look.

"I know these last few months have been hard for you and your family." Jace tried again. "With your wife sick and your son somewhere back east."

"My situation is no different than anyone else's." Owen threw up his hands. "Are you wanting me to confess that I blew up my own bank? What's the motivation for that?"

"No. I'm not saying that's what happened." Jace tried to hide his own irritation. "But it looks like someone was storing supplies inside the bank vault. And at this point, that's pretty good motivation for the explosion."

"Why would someone store supplies in the vault?"

"It's pretty clever, if you think about it. Houses have been periodically raided, grocery stores robbed, but who would ever think about robbing a bank vault when everything in it isn't worth anything anymore? But medical supplies, food supplies, and survival supplies. . . Those things are worth something."

"I'm not arguing that point, but I still don't see what any of this has to do with me. I told you, I don't know where that box came from, or any other supplies in the vault."

Lois Caddick, one of Owen's tellers, stepped into the station lobby with Aaron, her long brown hair pulled up in a messy bun and her customary business attire now replaced by a sleeveless dress and sandals. "Are you okay, Owen?"

"Still in shock, but yeah, I'm fine."

"If you'll excuse us for a moment, Owen," Jace said, "I'll make sure you have access to the bank so we can figure out together exactly what is missing."

Owen nodded, still clearly irritated as he stepped outside the station with Aaron.

"Lois, I appreciate your talking with me," Jace said, motioning her to Owen's now empty seat.

"I saw the bank," she said, fiddling with the tied belt at her waist. "I feel like I've been punched in the gut. I know it's been closed for months, but I worked there for five years. It makes no sense."

"I need to ask you a few questions."

"Of course," she said looking up at him. "Anything to find out who did this."

"Owen said that the two of you were the only ones with access to the vault."

"That's true."

"Did you ever store personal things in there?"

"I was just the teller and would have gotten fired for that, but what does it matter?" Lois frowned, as if she was trying to figure out where he was going with his questioning. "It's been months since I was in there."

"We found emergency supplies stored in the vault," Jace said, searching for signs of guilt in her expression.

Lois leaned forward. "And you believe that's what someone was after?"

"It makes sense, considering the value of those items right now."

Lois glanced toward the street, looking more confused than guilty. "Never thought I'd see the day where a first-aid kit is worth more than a stack of twenties. But if you really need to find out why they were in there. . ." Her voice lowered to just above a whisper. "I'd ask Owen about his wife."

Jace stepped away from the desk. "What do you mean?"

"Owen told me about the houses that were broken into. People going around stealing supplies they could sell on the black market, and it scared him. I'll be honest, it scared me too. Owen was a bit paranoid before all this happened, and had a stash of survival stuff, though I never saw it. It would make sense if he moved things into the vault. Nobody's trying to steal money anymore. And Nora, his wife, she's diabetic."

"Meaning. . ." Jace pressed.

"Your sister would know more than I do, but I know that Nora ran out of insulin a long time ago. I also know that homemade insulin is very difficult to make without a proper lab, and without electricity, impossible. But there are certain oral medications that can be used to help control blood sugar levels. If you can get them."

"On the black market," Jace said, the pieces finally starting to come together. And if she was right. . .

"If you're looking for motivation behind a stash of valuable things," Lois said, "it makes sense."

Jace stepped outside the station with Lois and assured her he was going to do everything in his power to find the truth. And that meant talking with Owen for a second time. The sun was starting to drop toward the horizon. In a couple of hours it would be dark, and he still had far too many questions.

"Finally," Owen said, starting toward the bank.

"Hold on," Jace said, calling him back.

"I thought we were done."

"Not quite." He stepped in front of the man then waited until Aaron and Lois were out of earshot. "Your wife is a diabetic, isn't she?"

"I'm done with your questions and backhanded accusations," Owen said, raising his voice.

"Owen, you need to calm down. We're on the same side."

"Are we? Because as far as I'm concerned, I don't have to listen to you. You and your family think you run this town, but I don't have to play by your rules."

Jace studied the man's expression, unsure of where the angry outburst was coming from. All the interactions he'd had with Owen over the past nine months had been cordial, with no traces of animosity.

Jace glanced over his shoulder. Their conversation was drawing attention from the crowd still huddled outside the bank. "Why don't we step back inside the station so we can talk in private?" he suggested.

"Forget it. I'm done talking," Owen said, stepping up within inches of Jace's face, his hands fisted beside him. He lowered his voice. "Crowley's Point. One hour."

Owen spun around on his heel and headed back across the street toward the bank.

Crowley's Point. One hour.

Owen's aggressive reaction made no sense, but neither did his last statement. Except Jace had seen more than just anger in the man's expression. He'd seen fear.

"Jace, is everything okay?"

Morgan walked up to him. Her khaki pants had a rip in the knee, and her white tank top looked like it had a bloodstain at the bottom. He stopped himself from pulling her into his arms, thankful she was alive.

"No. No, it's not." He ran his hand through his hair and frowned. Morgan had been through enough already today. She didn't need his troubles dumped on her as well. "But that doesn't matter. Are you okay? I heard you were there when the explosion hit, and your arm—"

"I'm fine," she said, shrugging off his concern. "It's just a few scratches. But we need to talk about the explosion. I might know who's involved."

CHAPTER TEN

MORGAN GLANCED down the street at what was left of the bank before stepping into the lobby of the police station in front of Jace. The scene was another eerie reminder of this post-apocalyptic nightmare.

"Have you found Frank?" she asked.

Jace offered her a chair, hesitating before leaning against his desk and answering her question. "Levi and several of the men are still out there. I came back when I heard the explosion. How's Noah?"

"I think he's okay," she said, sitting down. "Today's the day he spends with one of his friends. He wanted to go, and I thought it was better to keep his routine. Which meant thankfully he wasn't in town with me during the explosion."

"I'm glad to hear that. I've been worried about him."

"Me too." She tried to shake away the feelings of dread. That uncanny feeling of waiting for the next bad thing to hit the fan. Because something told her that whatever was going on was far from over. "Sometimes it feels like the darkness just keeps getting closer and closer."

"Like you're always waiting for the next bad thing to happen."

"Exactly. I know you're busy," she said, getting to the point of her visit, "but I think I saw something, or someone rather, in the crowd."

"Someone involved in the explosion?"

"It's possible." She bit her lip, wavering again on her decision to tell him.

"What is it, Morgan?"

"I could be wrong." She flicked away the fly buzzing around her ear. "I haven't seen him for over a year, but I thought I saw Tommy's brother, Ricky, in the crowd around the bank. He's been in and out of trouble with the law for as long as I can remember, and if he's back. . . Let's just say it's not for a good reason. It never is."

"When?"

"Right after the explosion. He was slipping through the crowd, and like I said, I'm not positive, but he was wearing a jacket, similar to one I've seen him in before, a yellow T-shirt, and a red ball cap. Ricky always wears ball caps."

"Okay." Jace glanced at his watch then steepled his fingers in front of him. "Let's go on the assumption he's back in Shadow Ridge. Why would he come here?"

She shook her head as she tried to work through the options. "I've never spent a lot of time with Ricky. He was the black sheep of the family, in and out of trouble over the years, only showing up when he needed something. We were used to him coming around every year or two, asking for money or a place to crash for a few weeks."

"You haven't seen him since before the Quake?"

"No." She wiped the beads of perspiration off the back of her neck, wishing for a breeze through the open windows to take the edge off the humidity. "Tommy never trusted Ricky because Ricky was always either hanging around the wrong types of people or in trouble himself."

"A man is dead, Morgan, and if there's a connection—if Ricky is involved in this—I need you to be careful."

She caught the worry in his eyes, but far more was inferred in his expression. His gaze was intense. . .expectant. . .and very personal. And she was terrified the walls around her heart were starting to crumble.

Morgan shifted in her seat, unable to shake off the uneasiness that had settled— both from the man sitting in front of her she was afraid she was falling for, and the realization Ricky might be back in town.

She cleared her throat. "I've never known him to be violent, and I don't think he would do anything to hurt me. But I could see him involved in the black market or drug running."

"I've met him, and I'm worried, Morgan. If Ricky is involved in this, I don't think you're safe."

Jace glanced at his watch again.

Morgan frowned. "Is everything okay?"

"Yeah." He clapped his hands against his thighs. "I just have to meet someone."

"That's fine. I need to go." She stood up and started toward the door. "I just felt like I should tell you about Ricky."

"Morgan, wait. I'm sorry I seem so distracted. I really do appreciate your coming by. If Ricky is in town, I needed to know."

She turned around, but Jace was back to being a lawman. Official, confident, and in charge.

"Don't worry about it." She forced a smile, confused by her own jumbled feelings. "You have a lot on your plate. Too much, really."

"Maybe, but please. Promise me you'll be careful until we find out who's behind this, especially if Ricky is involved."

"I promise."

She felt his hand press lightly against the small of her back as he walked her to the door. "And by the way, I hope I wasn't out of line to offer Noah some licorice this morning."

"No. I thought it was sweet. Literally."

"I'm glad."

She turned around and caught that familiar smile that reached his eyes.

"Listen." She swallowed hard, unsure how to handle the conflict simmering inside her. "You have to eat, so if you have time to get away for a little bit tonight, why don't you come for dinner and give it to him then. Any time."

Morgan regretted the impulsive invitation the moment it came out of her mouth. She didn't want to open her heart to him. Didn't want to fall for someone. But there was no way to take it back now. And neither could she ignore that mixed with the regret was an unexplainable anticipation of spending time with him.

"I'd like that actually. Thanks."

She forced a smile. "Great."

"One more thing," he said. "Do you have a photo of Ricky?"

"I'll have to look, but I should."

"Jace. . ."

Morgan looked up as Levi stepped into the station's lobby. She nodded at Levi, then started toward the door.

"Morgan, wait," Jace said again. "Would you mind staying a few more minutes? We might need your input."

"Of course, if you need me."

"Thanks," Jace said, ushering them both inside. "First of all, Levi, is everyone okay?"

"Yes. We left the horses and food as instructed, then followed Frank's trail, but we ended up losing him on the west ridge. We can head out again in the morning, but without a trail to follow, it's going to be almost impossible." Levi took off his hat and leaned back against the desk. "And he still has Keaton."

"Do you really think Frank's involved in Jeremiah's death?" Morgan asked.

Jace glanced at his brother, then back at her. "We found Frank near Whitman Trail. He'd taken Keaton as a hostage and made demands for supplies. He was planning to run."

Morgan shook her head. That wasn't the Frank she knew. The man who'd sacrificed so much for their town and his family and who never hesitated to answer a call for help. But she'd be the first to admit that the last year had changed everyone.

"I know he's been under a lot of stress," she said, "but it's still hard to imagine him taking a hostage and running. And Jeremiah. . . How does he fit into the picture? I can't believe Frank killed him. They were best friends."

"I know. It all seems implausible to me as well, but I can't ignore the connection." Jace turned to his brother. "Morgan came by to tell me she thought she saw Ricky at the scene of the explosion."

"Tommy's brother?" Levi asked.

Morgan nodded. "The last time I saw him he was headed to Washington State, but if you remember, he was always in and out of trouble. If he's here, it's either because he wants something, or because he's involved in something he shouldn't be."

"Do Frank and Ricky know each other?" Jace asked.

Morgan considered the idea. "They might have met, but Ricky didn't grow up here, and Frank's twenty years older with a family. I can't see that they would."

"There has to be a connection." Levi started to pace. "We need to send someone to talk to the county sheriff. See what we can find out from him."

"I'd like to, but these searches around Shadow Ridge are

dangerous enough. Matt and Grayson are already two days late from their last trip to Ft. Davis. I'm not sure I want to risk sending someone else out."

"They're always late."

"And I always worry," Jace said.

Levi stopped in front of him. "They'll be back. They always come back."

And if they didn't?

"Then what are we going to do?" Levi asked.

Morgan caught the tension in Jace's jaw. So much had been dumped on him due to his father's accident. He'd told her enough that she knew he'd never intended to stay in Shadow Ridge. If it weren't for the Quake, he wouldn't be here.

"I have a lead I need to follow up on," Jace finally answered. "Someone who asked to speak to me in private."

"I could go with you," Levi offered.

"Thank you, but for now, I want you to escort Morgan to her house and make sure she and Noah get there safely. Then I need you to set up security at the bank for overnight. The last thing we need is a second robbery by someone who thinks all that cash might be usable one day." Jace turned to Morgan. "I don't want to disappoint Noah, but I might not make it over tonight."

"It's okay. Really. I'll explain it to him if you can't come, and please, I'll be fine. I don't need an escort."

"Maybe not, but do it for me. So I won't worry. Please."

His dark eyes seemed to see right through her, boring toward the hidden spaces of her heart. Leaving her to question her feelings once again.

"Okay," she said, nodding. "And the dinner offer still stands. Any time."

CHAPTER ELEVEN

Crowley's Point was a crossroads a little less than a mile from the entrance of the McQuaid family ranch. Here the stunning view of rolling hills and mountain slopes was magnified, but Jace hardly noticed thanks to Owen's odd request.

He tied his horse fifty yards upwind from the point then made his way cautiously forward on foot. While Jace couldn't imagine the man setting him up, one thing was certain. Owen was scared of something. He'd seen the fear in his eyes.

He found Owen waiting for him beneath the shade of a juniper tree.

"Why the cloak and dagger, Owen?"

Owen stood and brushed off his pants. "They're watching me."

Jace set his hand on his gun and tilted his head. "Who's watching you?"

"I don't have time to play twenty questions, so I'm going to get right to the point," Owen said, walking toward him. "You asked about my wife. Yes, she's diabetic, which means she needs insulin."

"Okay. Has she run out?"

"Months ago, but there are other things she's been taking that seem to be working."

"For example?"

"Metformin. It's a pill used to treat type 2 diabetes, by helping to control blood sugar. "

"And where do you get that?"

Owen looked around, his hands twitching at his sides, still seemingly hesitant to answer.

"I'm not here to judge you for where you get your medicine," Jace said, "but I have one man dead, and an explosion I believe is connected."

Something rustled in the tall grass. Owen glanced past him to the other side of the empty stretch of road. A mule deer came into sight, stopped, then turned and ran deeper into the bush.

"You're the one who called me out here, Owen." Jace worked to keep the irritation out of his voice. "What's going on?"

"I've always been a bit of a survivalist. Stashing away supplies. I can't say that I ever thought the grid would go down, but you know what it's like living out here. I bet half the people in this town do the same thing."

"Not arguing that. And the supplies that were in the bank? They were yours?"

Owen shifted his stance then nodded. "Even my wife didn't know I'd moved them in the bank vault."

"What kind of stuff?" Jace asked.

"You name it, I had it. Survival stuff. Food, water purification tablets, flashlights, weapons, ammo. . ."

Jace shoved his hands into his pockets. "Why didn't you just tell me all of this in town?"

"Because I don't know who I can trust."

"Explain."

"I was buying medicine for Nora on the black market. The man who sold me the medicine somehow found out that I had a stash of supplies. I was worried they were going to search my house. So I moved the stuff to the bank vault. Three nights ago he and some other men came demanding more supplies. This time though, he didn't bring Nora's medicine. They ransacked my house, terrified my wife, and eventually left."

"Again. . ." Jace frowned, frustrated that he was hearing this for the first time. How was he supposed to help people when they wouldn't tell him what was going on? "Why didn't you tell me? I could have helped you."

"Could you?" Owen pulled a handkerchief from his pocket and wiped his brow. "They threatened to kill Nora if I told anyone they were there."

"Okay. We're going to figure this out. Do you know these men?"

"No. But if they discover I'm here talking with you and think I gave you information. . ."

"Would you recognize them?"

Owen hesitated. "They're not from here, but yeah, I think so. At least two of them."

"Do you know Ricky Addison?"

"Tommy's brother?"

Jace nodded. "Was he one of the men?"

"No," Owen said. "I'd recognize him."

"I'm going to have someone go to your house and get your wife." Jace removed his hat and brushed off a grasshopper that had landed on his pant leg. "I want you both to stay at my father's ranch for the next few days. And while you're there, you can work with my sister on some composite sketches. We need to know who's behind this."

"If I leave, or do anything out of the ordinary, they'll know something's up."

Jace frowned, wondering how things had gotten so complicated. But there had to be a solution. A way for him to keep the town safe and at the same time find out who was behind this.

"What do you normally do in the evenings?" Jace asked.

"I either stay home or spend an hour or two at the library."

"Then plan to meet my sister at the library tonight. She'll work with you to come up with some sketches of the men you saw."

Owen started for his horse, then stopped. "Who told you to ask about my wife?"

"I can't give you that information."

"It was Lois, wasn't it?"

"Like I said, I can't give out that information."

Owen swiped away the beaded moisture on his lip with his handkerchief. "Either way, you might want to look a bit deeper into her background."

"Meaning?" Jace asked.

"You brought up Ricky Addison. We both know he's a shady character who's nothing like his late brother. What you probably don't know is that he had a thing with Lois."

"What kind of a thing?" Jace pressed.

"I don't know the details, but let's just say they were pretty cozy when he came through."

As Owen started back toward town, Jace mounted Brisket and headed in the opposite direction toward the McQuaid River Ranch. The expansive views and abundant wildlife across two hundred acres had made it an oasis for the McQuaid family since the early 1900s. The ranch itself was surrounded by a combination of canyons, mountains, springs, and desert, most of which was untouched and wild.

He blew out a sharp breath, needing to use the short ride to calm his unease. The varied terrain had always managed to do that. From here, he could see everything from scrub, grassland,

and juniper savannas to the open hilltops and distant mountain slopes that were covered with piñon pine and oak. He'd grown up working the land, along with hunting and fishing. But now so much had changed.

He motioned for his horse to pick up the pace, knowing that the situation currently going on in town wasn't the only source of his anxiety. The last nine months had changed his father. He was no longer the head of their family or the law in Shadow Ridge.

As he neared the house he saw Margaret, his father's part-time caretaker, on the covered veranda of the two-story ranch house, knitting a purple afghan in the light of a lantern. The accordion doors that opened up beside her from the tiled living room onto the veranda allowed a panoramic view of the mountains and the sunset that would soon fade into darkness across the desert.

Jace sat down beside Margaret in one of the rocking chairs. "How's he doing?"

"About the same. Still feeling frustrated and useless." The old wooden rocking chair creaked as it moved with her stitches. "I hate to say this, but I'm starting to worry that he isn't going to come out of this. Grief might not have a timetable, but he needs to start moving forward."

The update, while not unexpected, still hurt.

"How are *you*?" Jace asked, looking at the older woman. Her hair had gone gray years ago and her face was lined with wrinkles and age marks, but the retired nurse had done what he'd believed to be impossible with regular physical therapy over the past few months. It was his father's heart he wasn't sure about. "You've taken on a lot, caring for my father."

"Your mother was my best friend. I can't tell you how much I miss her, but I know your father misses her even more. I'm doing this for her. And in a way, for me. Like your father, I need purpose."

He could relate to her response. He saw the far-reaching impact every day as people battled emptiness and confusion in this new world.

"What do I do, Margaret? I've tried to get him involved in my work," Jace said. "I've asked for his input and advice during this whole nightmare, but nothing has gotten him to see past what he's lost."

Margaret shook her head and dropped her project into her lap. "I wish I had an answer. All I know is that he needs more than just someone asking for his occasional input. He needs a purpose again."

Jace leaned forward, clasping his hands. "How do I do that? How do I help him find his purpose?"

"Garrett McQuaid has always been a one-man show, and incredibly good at what he does. He's been a husband, a lawman, a cowboy at heart, but except for you kids, everything that he knew and loved was ripped away from him. Getting back on his feet, literally, isn't going to be easy." Margaret went back to her knitting. "Go talk to him. He might not show it, but he loves it when you spend time with him."

Jace glanced up as the sun began to slip behind the horizon, leaving behind flames of yellow and orange. "Is Tess here? I need to talk to her."

"She's out in the barn with the horses. This morning really upset her. Seeing Jeremiah's body."

"I know." Jace shook his head, feeling as if he'd let everyone around him down by not stopping this.

"But she'll be okay. She's stronger than you think," Margaret continued. "And your father isn't the only one who needs a purpose."

"I just worry about her," Jace said, standing up. "One more thing. Do you ever sell the candy you make?"

"I trade it sometimes."

"Like the licorice?"

"Yes, though people want the sugar I make from my sugar beets more than anything else."

"Do you sell it at the market?" he asked.

"I usually have someone there sell it for me. It helps supplement my garden."

Necessity had driven the town to hold a weekly market in town where people traded everything from household goods, to food items, to animals. And although he and Levi had been forced to step in more than once to stop a fight, overall, the system worked. Jace's mind shifted back to the tobacco he'd found at the crime scene and then again in Frank's barn. But Levi was right. It could have come from anywhere.

Margaret stopped rocking. "Is everything okay?"

"Yeah. I'm just trying to figure some things out."

"You're doing a good job, Jace. Don't forget that."

He nodded his thanks, then headed toward the front door. Darkness had already settled in when he stepped into the living room. A candle sat beside an uneaten tray of soup and homemade bread. His father's German shepherd, Ranger, got up from beside his father's chair.

Jace knelt down and rubbed the back of his neck. "Hey, Ranger. How are you doin', sweet boy?"

Ranger nuzzled his nose against Jace's leg, clearly enjoying the attention.

Jace sat down on the chair next to his father and picked up the open book sitting on the end table between them. "Louis L'Amour. I remember when you used to read these."

"Tess thought I might like to read through them again."

Jace studied his father's profile. Along with his ability to fight, he'd lost at least thirty pounds over the past few months. Margaret had been faithful about coming and doing physical therapy with him during the week, but even that hadn't been enough. Margaret was right. He'd lost his purpose.

"I need your advice on something, Dad," Jace finally said.

"You don't need my advice." His father clasped his hands in front of him. "Everyone who stops by tells me you're doing a fantastic job. Despite your initial reluctance to lead this town, you're exactly what was needed."

"I'm not sure I'm really doing a good job." Jace glanced at the open window. The blue curtains rustled in the breeze that wasn't enough to combat the heat. "Jeremiah Daniels is dead."

His father leaned forward. "What happened?"

"I'm not sure yet. Someone broke into the community storehouse and stole a good portion of the food."

"Do you know who's behind this?"

"The evidence points to Frank," Jace said.

"Frank Savage?"

Jace nodded.

"Are you sure? I've always known Frank to be a decent man."

Jace hesitated. "People change."

"So what do you need from me?" his father asked, not seeming to make the connection.

"I know how to interrogate someone and make them talk," Jace said. "That's what I'm good at. But investigating a murder is different, especially since I feel like my hands are tied. I don't have databases, forensics, or external experts. Really, I have no resources at all."

His dad let out a low chuckle. "Forensics has been around for longer than you think. They might not have used DNA profiling or firearm analysis, but the ancient Greeks and Romans used forms of basic forensics, particularly in their study of toxins. The Chinese have been studying dead bodies for signs of foul play for hundreds of years. The bottom line is that criminal profiling and the examination of crime scenes is nothing new."

"I suppose you have a point," Jace admitted.

"Modern forensics might aid in the investigation, but whether you're interrogating a suspect or searching a crime scene, you're simply looking to discover the truth. A murder investigation is no different."

The candlelight cast shadows on the wall and caught the intensity in his father's face. Garrett McQuaid had been good at his job, and he'd never relied on modern-day technology.

"Walk me through what happened," his father said.

Jace gave him a brief overview of the day's events, starting with finding Jeremiah's body in the warehouse, and then the hostage situation.

"Wait a minute." His father held up his hand and stopped Jace midsentence. "You're telling me that Frank took a hostage? I'm having a hard time buying that."

"I wouldn't have believed it either, except I was there, Dad. I saw him."

"I guess it's possible." His father reached down and rubbed the leg Jace knew still bothered him.

Jace nodded. "Morgan believes she saw Tommy's brother, Ricky, at the explosion. I'm going to try and find out if he might be involved as well."

"And the connection behind of all of these random pieces?"

Jace paused as he tried to make sense in his own mind. "I think this could somehow be connected to the black market trade, but I don't have enough evidence yet."

"Do you want my advice?"

Jace nodded. "Always."

"What are the rules of an interrogation?"

Jace braced his hands against his thighs, not sure where the conversation was going. "Be prepared, methodical, and at times sympathetic."

"And dismiss any preconceived ideas."

"You think that's what I'm doing?"

"Only you can answer that, but it's too easy to get tunnel vision and miss what's going on around you."

Ranger came up and brushed against his leg, begging for attention. Jace rubbed the dog's head. "I need you to come back, Dad."

His father straightened out his leg. "I walk to the barn every day, but that's about it. I couldn't even get to town."

"You're strong enough to ride again," Jace said.

"Not yet, and even if I did ride to town, then what? I don't have the stamina anymore."

"That could change. You could work up to it."

His dad grasped the arms of the chair. "I've had to accept where I am, and you're going to need to do that as well."

Jace frowned. It was like this every time he came out to the ranch to see his dad. Progress was minimal because he refused to push himself. A part of Jace understood the lack of motivation. His father had lost his wife, his career, and had limited use of his legs. The losses had taken their toll.

His father grabbed his cane and started pacing, his limp obvious as he worked to stretch the muscles. "Tess told me you've been seeing a lot of Morgan."

"Changing the subject?" Jace asked.

His father turned around. "I'd always rather talk about you than me."

"I'm just doing my job."

"Is it your job to take her some of Margaret's raspberry jam?" His father's grin surprised him, but it quickly faded. "All I'm saying is you need someone like Morgan. Sometimes a good woman only comes around once in a lifetime."

Jace caught the pain in his father's voice. The deep-seated ache of having lost the love of his life.

"Maybe, but I'm not looking for a relationship. Besides, Morgan would never leave Shadow Ridge, and I don't plan to stay here forever."

"And what happens if there isn't an end to this?" His father sat back down. "What if this is our permanent reality?"

"It won't be. It can't be."

Could it?

Jace looked away, not completely able to imagine that future. But he also knew that he was really trying to talk himself out of his growing feelings toward Morgan. Trying to convince himself that all of this was temporary.

"I have an apartment back in Atlanta."

"What's going to happen to that once you're shipped off again? One day you're going to have to stop running, Son."

Jace stared at the flicking candle, unsure of how they'd gotten so off track with their conversation. He had yet to tell his father he'd left the military. It was a conversation that had never come up. A conversation he'd not wanted to come up.

"All I know is I can't imagine staying here forever."

His father's gaze seemed to pierce right through him. "Sometimes what you've been looking for your whole life turns out to be what you've been frantically running away from."

The curtain flapped in the breeze of the open window. A moth flitted around the edges of the open flame. Outside was the desert, a place that had always pulled at him. But he could only take so much solitude, and he'd never been able to shake the need to keep moving.

Not like Morgan. No. She'd managed to find peace in this place, a peace in the chaos of life, without needing to run. Maybe he'd been wrong about her. Maybe he was just trying to fill a void.

"I've got to go make some arrangements with Tess for tonight," Jace said, standing up and ignoring his conflicted thoughts for the moment.

"Just don't close your heart off to love. Having somebody by your side in the midst of hardship is one of the best things there is."

Jace told his father goodnight, then let Ranger follow him out to the veranda. He picked up the dog's favorite ball and threw it across the grass in the moonlight. Ranger took off like a lightning bolt, then promptly turned around and brought it back.

"You would do this all night, wouldn't you, boy." He threw the ball again then looked up at the endless canopy of stars. West Texas had always been the place he came back to, but his soul was too restless to stay put in one place. It was one of the reasons why he decided to join the military. It fed that restless spirit, never giving him time to think. He just did what he was told.

The last nine months had given him too much time to think.

No, Shadow Ridge couldn't be where he settled down permanently. Someday this would all be over and he could go back to living his life. But what if his father was right? What if closing his heart to love ended up costing him everything?

CHAPTER TWELVE

JACE STEPPED onto Morgan's front porch, wondering if he should be dropping by so late. Her house sat at the edge of town on the end of a quiet street and backed up against several acres where Tommy had built the greenhouses. Yellow light from the living room fireplace shone through the front windows, and he could smell the garlic and onions from the simmering stew she'd promised to cook. He'd spent the last two hours in town coordinating another search for tomorrow, arranging the bank's clean up and security, and getting Tess set up to work with Owen on sketches of their suspects.

He hesitated a moment longer, then knocked.

"Hey," he said, once she'd opened the door.

"Hey."

"I know it's late, but you said if the light was on. . ." He stopped, unable to ignore how stunning she looked with the yellow glow of the firelight behind her. She'd let down her hair, so her dark waves brushed just past her shoulders, and there was a hint of a smile on her lips. Enough for him to believe she might even be happy to see him.

"It's fine," she said, motioning him inside. "But you didn't have to take the time to stop by for Noah's sake. I know there's so much going on right now."

"Yes, there is, but I'm a man of my word." He held up the small bag of candy. "There's a little boy waiting for some licorice, but I also understood that dinner was in the deal for me."

"He actually wouldn't let me forget that." She let out a low laugh. "He made me promise I would wait up for you if he fell asleep and that I needed to give you an extra helping of rabbit stew."

"He's a sweet boy," Jace said.

"Keeping up with him is a full-time job, though I wouldn't want it any other way."

Jace followed her into the tiled living room with its wood furniture, colorful blankets,

and rugs, all adding to the rustic, cozy feel of the room. Family photos sat lined up on the fireplace, and a guitar case sat propped up in the far corner of the room next to a piano.

"Do you play?" he asked.

"The guitar, not the piano. Tommy and I. . ." Her gaze dropped. "We used to play together. He was really good on the piano."

"I didn't know about your music abilities, but I do know about your cooking. I'm sure Noah was right about your rabbit stew being the best. It smells amazing." Jace turned toward the kitchen, needing to shift the direction of the conversation. "How is he?"

"He seems okay. Definitely better. I'm watching him closely. He hung out with his friend, then I took him to the park and let him burn off some energy. We also went and visited Miss Dorothy and her chickens. Hope told me to try to keep things as normal as possible, but I don't know. He's been through so much these past few months and lost so much. . ."

"He's resilient."

Morgan glanced toward the hallway. "Maybe, but no matter how normal I try to make life for him, this. . ." She pointed to the cast-iron pot hanging in the fireplace and the lit candles. "This isn't normal. Not only do I have to worry about food and schooling, my son saw the body of someone who'd been murdered today." She dropped her hands to her sides. "I'm sorry. You didn't come over to hear my problems."

He reached out and squeezed her hand, then quickly pulled back. No. He was playing with fire and he knew it.

"Is there anything I can do?" he asked, trying to keep any hint of intimacy from his voice.

She shook her head. "All I can really do is live one day at a time and try not to worry about tomorrow."

"Today has enough trouble," he said.

"Jesus certainly was right. Though. . ." She glanced up at him. "There are rumors going around town about what's out there. Chaos. . .unrest. . .lawlessness. I'm not sure if we're ready for what's coming next."

"Mom!" Noah ran into the living room carrying a couple books. "Is he here?"

Morgan stepped aside. "See for yourself."

Jace held up the paper bag. "I promised someone licorice. Now who was that?"

"Me!" Noah squealed.

Morgan laughed. "You know you're going to spoil him."

"Nothing wrong with that every once in a while," Jace said. "Though I guess I could've brought you both a pound of carrots instead."

Noah wrinkled his nose.

"I suppose the licorice will have to do, then."

"You never told me where you got it," Morgan said, ushering him toward the bar stools that lined the counter dividing the living room from the kitchen.

Jace grinned as he settled onto one of the stools. "So you have a sweet tooth as well?"

"She does," Noah said.

"I'll have to remember that." Jace shot Noah a smile. "Every Sunday, Margaret brings me a sample of something she's made. This week it happened to be homemade licorice."

"Why don't you show him what you're coloring," Morgan said to Noah, "and I'll dish up the stew."

Noah jumped up next to Jace on one of the stools, then turned the drawing around and held it up. "It's an airplane."

"That's pretty cool," Jace said.

"Thanks."

"And that's your book on airplanes?" Jace asked, pointing.

Noah handed him the book. "My grandma and grandpa gave it to me before the planes stopped flying."

Jace flipped through some of the brightly colored pages that reminded him just how much the world had changed. No airplanes flying overhead. No streaming movies or on-line shopping. . .

Noah grinned up at him. "Can I have a piece of candy before dinner?"

Jace glanced at Morgan, who was ladling the stew into bowls. She nodded.

"One." He pulled out a piece of the soft black candy. "Have you ever been on a plane?"

"I went once to see my grandma and grandpa. They live in Arkansas." Noah popped the candy into his mouth, then grabbed a blue marker. "Do you like to fly?"

"I do, actually. I even have my own flying machine."

Noah stopped coloring. "You have an airplane?"

"Not exactly. I have a paraglider."

Noah frowned, looking a little less impressed. Apparently a paraglider didn't sound nearly as exciting as an airplane. "A what?"

"It's like flying with the birds. Soaring over the land with no motor. Just layers of fabric that are connected to a harness."

Noah scrunched his lips together. "How does it fly without a motor?"

"The wind carries you."

Noah still didn't look impressed.

"Can I draw you a picture of one?" Jace asked.

Noah pushed the pad of paper and his markers toward Jace, who started drawing a rough sketch of a paraglider.

"There's what's called a large paraglider wing," Jace said, "and it's attached by strong lines that hold you up in the harness."

"Are you alone when you fly?"

"I could take someone with me and fly tandem, but most of the time I do it alone."

"What's tandem?" Noah asked.

"Tandem means more than one person," Morgan said as she set two of the bowls on the counter.

Noah ran to a bookshelf, put his hands on his hips for a moment, then pulled out a book.

He ran back to the counter while Morgan went to get the rest of the food.

"Like this?" he asked. "A hot air balloon?"

"It's very similar, though my paraglider fits in a bag and I carry it in the back of my truck."

Noah's eyes widened, though Jace still wasn't sure if he was impressed or simply trying to understand the concept.

"Are you joking with me?" Noah finally asked.

"No, and I'll tell you what. . .one of these days, if it's okay with your mom, I'll take you flying with me."

Noah leaned forward. "I don't think my mom would let me do that. What if you get lost because you don't have a pilot?"

Jace reached in and pulled his compass out of his pocket. "My father gave this to me when I was sixteen. He said if I ever got lost it would help me find my way home."

"Have you ever gotten lost?"

For some reason the question took Jace by surprise. Sometimes getting lost had nothing to do with direction. Sometimes it had everything to do with how he felt on the inside.

"I haven't yet," Jace said, slipping it back into his pocket. "But I carry it because it reminds me that I always have a place to come home to."

Noah pulled out a photo from his back pocket and unfolded it. "My mom gave me this picture so I don't forget what my dad looks like. Sometimes it's hard to remember."

"You look a lot like your father," Jace said.

Noah folded up the photo then put it back in his pocket. "Mom?"

"Yeah, babe."

"Can we eat?"

She rested her hands on her hips and smiled. "I thought you spoiled your dinner with licorice."

"Just one." Noah stuck out his black tongue. "Can I pray?"

"Of course."

Noah grabbed his mom and Jace's hands, waited for them to hold hands, then bowed his head.

Jace felt Morgan's fingers press against his as Noah prayed for the food, for him and Morgan, for the town, for Jeremiah's family. Sitting here together, the three of them felt like. . .like family.

Family.

The thought surprised Jace as Noah said amen. He wasn't looking for a family of his own. He was doing what he had to do until this nightmare was over. Surviving. But what if he found someone to love in the process?

"Thank you, Noah," Morgan said.

He looked at Morgan. No matter how hard he'd tried to ignore his feelings, she'd managed to move in and capture his heart. But those were feelings he wasn't ready to sort out. Not now. For now, he just needed to make sure she stayed safe while he figured out what was going on in town.

Sometimes a good woman only comes around once in a lifetime.

His father's words resurfaced, but he pushed them back and dug into his stew.

"You were right, Noah," Jace said, scooping up another bite. "This is the best rabbit stew I've ever had."

"I told you."

Jace listened as Noah chatted about everything from playing Legos with his friends to being chased by one of Dorothy's chickens.

Family.

The word wouldn't let him go. He wanted that. One day. But his career had put him in situations he'd never wanted to drag a family into. What if all of this was his permanent reality?

What if it wasn't?

Or did it even matter?

Noah set his spoon in his empty bowl, then leaned forward. "Can I have some more licorice?"

"One more piece tonight, then head off to brush your teeth and get ready for bed."

Noah popped a licorice into his mouth. "Mom, can I go flying in his para. . .para. . ."

"Paraglider," Jace finished for him.

"I'll think about it, but right now, it's time for bed."

"It can fly without a motor," Noah said, finally sounding amazed by the idea. "And you can fly like a bird."

"Sounds a bit. . ." Morgan looked at Jace. "Terrifying, but in the meantime. . ."

Noah frowned. "Off to bed."

Morgan kissed him on the forehead. "That's right."

"Thank you for the licorice," Noah said. He jumped down off the stool and grabbed his books and lantern before running down the hallway.

"He's definitely a lot better tonight," Jace said.

"He is, and I'm grateful." Morgan picked up the bowls and set them in the sink. "I just worry about the long-term effects from all of this."

He nodded, understanding firsthand the truth of her statement. Even if this was all over tomorrow, there would still be consequences that would have to be dealt with.

She pulled something out of one of the kitchen drawers and handed it to him. "Before I forget. It's a photo of Ricky."

"Thank you." He slid it into his back pocket. "This will help, though I do have a question about Ricky."

"Sure."

"Do you know if he had a relationship with Lois Caddick?"

"From the bank?" Morgan's eyes widened. "It would surprise me, though I really don't know. Ricky always came and went without talking much about his personal life. What are you thinking?"

"Someone told me they had been involved. And if he is in town, there's a good possibility that she's seen him."

"Sounds like it's worth looking into."

"I plan on it, though at this point, there's still no proof that Ricky's involved in any of this."

"Maybe not, but trouble always seems to follow him."

Morgan turned back to the counter. "Would you like some coffee?"

Jace glanced at his watch. "I probably should head back out. I need to check on the security at the bank, and then—"

"You're carrying a heavy load, Jace McQuaid." She turned around, frowning at his response. "You can't work twenty-four seven and expect to keep going. When's the last time you took a day off and did something just for fun?"

Jace hesitated at the question. Fun wasn't exactly a part of his vocabulary. Not anymore, anyway.

Morgan braced her hands against the counter in front of him. "Well?"

"Fun is overrated," he said, copping out.

"How much sleep do you usually get?" she fired back.

"Levi and I switch night shifts, which helps."

"That doesn't answer my question."

"Four. . .maybe five hours."

Her shoulders slumped as she caught his gaze. "I worry about you, taking on the responsibility of the entire town. It's too much for one person. Maybe you can delegate more—"

"I'm trying. I really am." He got up from the stool and headed into the kitchen. "The truth is that we don't live in a safe world anymore. Haven't for a long time. That's the reality. What's your system?"

"For dishes? Wash in soap and a little bleach, double rinse, then drain, but I can do this later."

"Nope," he said, starting the process. "See how great delegating is?"

She laughed, and some of the tension between them seemed to evaporate. Her questions had been legitimate, but so were his answers. All he could do was deal the best he could with each day. A comfortable silence settled between them as they washed the dishes. A seemingly mundane task that somehow felt as if they'd done it together a hundred times.

"I am worried about your being here by yourself," he said, handing her another dish. "And no, if I'm honest, I don't worry about all the single women in town as much as I worry about you."

He caught her blush in the candlelight, but didn't miss the frown either. "I'm not leaving my home, Jace. There's been enough disruption for Noah. I've done everything I can to secure the house. I have several guns locked up, and I know how to use them."

"What if that's not enough?" Jace asked. "You could stay out at my dad's ranch. He's got several ranch hands who keep an eye on the house and the property."

She shook her head. "I'm learning there are no guarantees in life, Jace. All we can do is our best, and then leave the rest to God. I'll be fine here."

Jace turned away, frustrated at her stubbornness. Frustrated that her safety mattered so much to him. Frustrated that she was right.

"You blame God for all this, don't you?" she asked.

He glanced at her, surprised by the direct question. Uncomfortable that she could read him and the issue he was wrestling with. "Yeah. . .sometimes, it's hard not to."

"I get it," she continued. "I really do. When Tommy died, I struggled with anger because I knew God could have stopped it. You know even more than I do that this world is filled with sin and hurt. Somehow we have to remember that despite all the bad things that happen, God is still good. And He's still right here in the middle of the mess. A mess all too often of man's own making."

. . .

He wanted to tell her that she was wrong. That his faith hadn't struggled in this storm, because he was strong enough to face the doubts head on.

Except none of that was true.

"Thank you," he said, finally picking up another bowl.

"For what?"

"For not being afraid to challenge me. For reminding me of what's truly important."

"I'm talking to myself as well." She took the bowl from him, rinsed it, and set it in the dishrack. "Would it make you feel better if I asked Hope to stay here for a few days? At least until you figure out what's going on. She'd still be close to the clinic, and maybe you'd worry less."

He smiled. "You don't mind?"

"I'll talk to her if it will stop you from pestering me." She grinned, managing to pass through another hard layer of his wall.

He finished washing the last bowl, then handed it to her. "You know I'm concerned about this town, but being here with you. . .this has nothing to do with my job."

"I know." Her words were barely above a whisper as she looked up at him.

He turned to face her, caught the light in her eyes reflecting off the candles. He hadn't meant to fall for her. She was both a fiery spirit and a gentle soul—a captivating combination that had managed to draw in his heart. Maybe it was just a web of emotions he was caught up in.

Or maybe he was falling in love.

He brushed his hands against hers then laced their fingers together, surprised when she didn't pull away. "I've tried really hard to ignore what I feel, but I'm falling for you, Morgan."

She looked down at their hands and let out a quick breath. His own gaze shifted to her lips. He wished he could read her mind, or at least have some clue whether or not she was feeling the same thing he was.

"What are you thinking?" he finally asked.

"Honestly, I don't know."

"I didn't plan this, but no matter how hard I try not to, every time I see you, I fall a little harder."

"Do you want me to be honest?" she asked.

"Definitely."

"I'm afraid of a lot of things, but mainly that you're here because you feel sorry for me."

Jace shook his head. "I don't feel sorry for you. I just think we're good together. You make me smile. You challenge me and make me want to be a better man. And Noah. . . He's captured my heart as well."

"But what happens when life gets back to normal? What happens when you can leave here?" Her smile was gone, but she didn't pull away from him. "When you realize you're saddled with me and Noah? I can't let that happen."

"I can't ever see myself feeling regret over being *saddled* with you." He studied her dark eyes and long lashes in the glow of the candlelight, and the freckles dusting her flushed cheeks. This time he knew he was speaking from his heart. "And I don't think things going back to normal will change how I feel. Maybe I wouldn't feel this way if the situation were different. If life hadn't changed drastically. But it did, and I'm here, and I can't deny how I feel any longer."

"I just don't know how to open up my heart again. I'm so afraid of losing someone I love, and your job doesn't help."

He pulled her hands against his chest, searching her eyes for confirmation that he wasn't the only one feeling this way. She reached up and kissed him—and in that one kiss managed to echo everything he was feeling.

She pressed her fingertips against his chest, then took a step back. "Jace, we need to talk about this. About us. I don't think this can—"

A sharp knock on the door interrupted whatever she was wanting to say.

Jace hesitated, then went to open the door. Gideon stood on the porch.

"Gideon. What's going on?"

"There's been a break-in at the clinic. Levi asked me to come get you."

"Was Hope there?"

Gideon nodded. "I think she's okay. I know she sprained her ankle."

Jace turned back to Morgan.

"I'll be fine," she said, hurrying him out the door. "Just let me know what's going on when you can."

Jace nodded. "Lock the door behind you."

Morgan felt the guilt sweep through her as she leaned against the closed door. What in the world had she been thinking in kissing Jace McQuaid? She had no intention of opening her heart to someone else. Her first and only priority was keeping Noah safe. And Jace. . . She'd known for weeks that he had feelings for her, and yet while she'd done nothing to encourage him, neither had she done anything to discourage him.

Having Jace in her house tonight, seeing Noah smiling around him, had brought to the surface a deep yearning inside of her for something normal. For family, and someone to keep her safe. But those weren't reasons to start a relationship.

Working to control her confused emotions, Morgan crossed the living room and stopped in front of the hidden closet her husband had built. Vertical shiplap panels hid both the door and the lock, making it the perfect secure place for guns and other valuables. She opened it up and pulled out one of Tommy's rifles. She'd worry about her heart later. Whatever was going on out there. . .she was going to be ready.

CHAPTER THIRTEEN

Jace and Gideon started at a fast trot down Morgan's drive, then headed north toward Main Street in the moonlight.

"Do you know what happened?" Jace asked.

"Not really," Gideon said. "Just that someone broke into the clinic while your sister was still there. Your brother didn't want to leave her alone."

"I'm glad you came and got me," Jace said, "though you're out late."

"My mom's suffering from a migraine. She asked me to see if Dr. Hope had anything that might help."

Jace nodded, trying not to worry during the short time it took to get to the clinic, but Morgan was right. The load he was carrying did feel heavy, and sometimes he blamed God. He glanced up at the Milky Way. While his belief in a creator God had never wavered, it was too easy to base faith on circumstances. Hard to ignore feelings that God seemed indifferent toward everything happening.

With the sun already down, Main Street was dark except for a few lanterns glowing in the windows. Six months ago, the town had voted on a curfew. Except for emergencies and town gatherings, people were encouraged to be in their homes after dark. It kept his job of patrolling the streets easier and had, in part, helped curb crime.

"Hope, Gideon said you were hurt," Jace said, quickly dismounting in front of the clinic and hurrying toward his sister who was sitting on the curb. Levi hovered over her.

"It's just my ankle. It's a little sore, but I don't think it's too bad." Hope shook her head. "I'm mainly shaken. Whoever was in there knocked me down. I think I surprised them as much as they surprised me."

"Do you have any idea who it was?"

"No." Hope shook her head. "I'm sorry. I didn't see their faces, and they were gone before I could pick up my flashlight."

The sound of breaking glass jerked Jace's attention back to the clinic.

"Someone's still in there," he said, grabbing his flashlight from his saddlebag.

"I cleared the clinic when I first got here," Levi said, "but I didn't want to leave Hope out here alone. It's possible they were hiding and I missed them."

"Levi, Gideon, stay with her while I go inside."

Jace flipped on his flashlight and headed into the clinic. Shadows in the waiting room from the moonlight filtered in through the windows, but he saw no signs of anyone here. He slowly made his way through the rest of the clinic. Glass crunched under his feet as he walked down the hallway. He stopped at the busted back door window and felt a breeze through the opening. This had to have been their entry point.

A scraping noise shifted his attention to one of the exam rooms on the west side. Jace opened up the door to the room. The small window above the exam bed was open, but there wasn't enough room for a person to go through it. Jace's flash-light caught movement on the ground. He stumbled past a rolling chair as green eyes flashed at him. The cat meowed, then jumped to the windowsill and disappeared into the darkness.

Heart pounding from the unexpected adrenaline rush, Jace turned toward the back of the clinic. The cat hadn't left the exam room. And certainly hadn't broken the window. No. Someone was definitely still inside. He kept moving systematically through the clinic, stopping again at the open door of the supply room. Jace shone his light on the lock that had been jimmied, and frowned. The medical supplies that were kept in open storage bins were now strewn across the floor. Someone had been in here looking for something.

Jace heard the back door open. He ran out of the supply room as someone sprinted into the alley behind the clinic. Jace took off after the hooded figure, shouting for them to stop. The alley ran between Main Street stores and a long row of houses. He shouted again for the shadowy figure to stop as he pressed to close the distance between them. Moonlight streamed across the road as Jace followed the figure across the street then toward the back of the library.

Jace stopped at the edge of the gravel parking lot unsure of which way the man had gone. He watched for movement. The wind rustled through the row of trees, but he had no idea which way he'd gone.

He'd lost him.

Irritation twisted through him. Searching in the dark would be impossible. What frustrated him, though, was that he didn't even have a description of the person. From the build he assumed it was a man, but beyond that he had no idea.

Hope stood up as Jace walked back to the clinic. "What happened?"

"Someone was inside. They broke into your supply room."

Hope frowned. "I keep a lot of things locked up in there,

and I can't afford to lose anything. My resources are so diminished right now. If it wasn't for Max and the herbal home remedies he gives me, I'd pretty much have nothing."

"Levi, you and Gideon go find a board and cover the back door where the window's broken. We need to make sure this place is as secure as possible."

"I'm not sure it matters. It didn't stop them this time," Hope said, putting some pressure on her foot and wincing.

Jace reached for her. "Hope, stop. I don't think you should be walking on that ankle."

"Last time I looked, I was the doctor," his sister said, waving him off. "I'll be fine."

Jace looked to Levi, but his brother just held up his hands. "I'm staying out of this one."

"Fine. What do you need?" Jace asked.

"I need to see what was taken. It might give us some answers. And I'll get your mother some lavender oil, Gideon. That should help."

"And something for your foot," Jace said.

"I think I still have a couple instant ice packs."

Jace helped her to the small room in the back where she insisted on going through all the cabinets and drawers.

"This is so frustrating," she said, pulling out an empty bin. "But I shouldn't be surprised. Honestly, I've expected something like this to happen."

"The fact that you've kept your door open at all is a testament to both the townspeople and to you," Jace said.

Hope turned around, then held up her hands. "There are quite a few first-aid items missing. . .bandages, alcohol, and some burn ointment, but what concerns me most is that they also took about a third of what was left of my prescription medicines."

That made sense. It was possible that someone involved in

the explosion had been injured, and the prescription meds would sell quickly on the black market.

"You think my father's behind this."

Jace turned around as Gideon stepped into the doorway.

"I don't know who broke in here," Jace said.

Gideon's expression darkened. "You told me that sometimes people feel so trapped that they don't know which way is up. I've seen that. Everything that's happened since the Quake seems to have brought out the best and the worst in people."

"Is there something you haven't told me, Gideon?"

Jace caught the boy's gaze for a moment before Gideon looked away.

"Gideon?"

Gideon hesitated again before he said anything. "I'm the one who stole the extra grain bags you found in our barn."

"Why?" Hope asked.

"I was planning to sell them."

"For more tobacco?" Jace asked.

Gideon nodded. "That and other things. I know it was wrong. I just. . . I didn't think anyone would notice a few bags missing."

"What about the empty box of explosives?" Jace asked. "It was lying near the grain. You could have gotten a lot for what was inside."

"I swear I don't know anything about that," Gideon said. "It wasn't there when I hid the grain bags."

Jace pulled out the photo Morgan had given him from his back pocket. "You told me that a guy sold you the tobacco behind the school."

Gideon nodded.

Jace held up the photo of Ricky. "Do you recognize this man?"

Gideon studied it for a moment, then shook his head. "No."

"What about this guy?" Jace showed him the sketch of Owen's supplier that Tess had come up with.

Gideon hesitated. "It could be him."

"And you don't know his name?"

"No. I'm sorry."

"What do we do?" Hope asked.

"I think we have to stick with our plan," Jace said. "As soon as it's light, we start looking for Frank again. He's gonna need to be near water and a source of food, which should narrow things down. With this photo and the sketches from Tess, I'm hoping we can identify who's involved in this. But for now, we all need to get some rest."

Hope handed Gideon a small vial of lavender oil. "The directions are on it. It should help your mom's migraines."

"Thank you." Gideon's gaze dropped. "Am I in trouble?"

"Yes, but I want you to get back home," Jace said. "Your mother needs you."

Gideon nodded. The defiance Jace had seen earlier in the boy's gaze was gone.

"There is one other thing," Jace said, turning to his sister. "I'd like for you to stay with Morgan the next few nights. Just until we figure out what's going on. I'm worried about both of you being alone."

Hope picked up the instant icepack she'd pulled out of one of the bins. "You worry too much, Jace. I know that's your job, but I'll be okay. I can shoot as well as any crook who might show up. . .maybe better."

Jace frowned.

"You're serious, aren't you?" she asked.

He glanced at her foot. "You lost that round, and it could have been worse. I just don't want to take any chances."

"Fine." Hope said, starting for the door. "Does Morgan know about this plan of yours?"

Jace hesitated. "I had dinner with her tonight."

"Really."

"It's not what you think," he rushed on. "I promised to bring Noah some licorice, and she invited me for dinner."

"Okay. That sounds like nothing." Hope smiled at him.

"Come on," Jace said, shining his flashlight back toward the hall and ignoring her grin. "I'll give you a ride to Morgan's on Brisket so you won't have to walk."

Jace helped his sister out of the clinic, trying to forget about Morgan's kiss and whatever she'd been about to say before Gideon knocked on the door. He hadn't missed the doubt and confusion in her eyes. Nor could he shake off the worry that kissing her had been a mistake.

CHAPTER FOURTEEN

JACE HEADED BACK down Morgan's drive after dropping off his sister, then changed his plan. No. He wasn't going to leave. Not tonight. He knew that both Morgan and Hope had experience with guns, but with all the break-ins, he was concerned about their safety. He put Brisket inside a fenced enclosure nearby, then settled into one of the abandoned cars along the street where he could watch the house.

Depression fell on him like a blanket trying to smother him. Most of the time he was able to keep the demons at bay. But there were times, like tonight, when he felt like everything was out of control. When he couldn't figure out what he was missing. When he felt like he was a lone man trying to stand in the middle of the rapids. God might've called people like Moses who argued with the Almighty about his abilities, but still. . . How was he supposed to keep going when he felt that he had nothing left inside of him?

He closed his eyes and let his mind wander. Took in a deep breath and tried to calm this shattering of nerves. But instead of finding peace, he was there again, sitting in the dimmed light of the interrogation room. Responsible for getting the answers they needed in order to stop another attack.

Jace rubbed the back of his neck, trying to work out the tension. He'd always wanted to be a warrior and had worn his uniform with pride. In his job, information he uncovered could be just as valuable as firepower. It gave them the advantage to stop attacks and save lives.

But what happened when he couldn't get that information? What happened when he couldn't save those he was responsible for?

His fingers tapped against the steering wheel, trying to move the pieces of the puzzle around to make sense of the current situation. Frank had anger issues. Everyone knew that. He'd grown up in the oil fields and was gruff and rough around the edges. But everyone who knew him also knew that he was a teddy bear inside. And as far as Jace was concerned, the man's volunteering was his way of giving back to the town. So what had changed? And why?

Jace let out a sharp huff of air, wishing he could escape the constant whisperings in his head, the ones that told him he was failing to protect this town. He'd returned to Shadow Ridge to try and find peace with what had happened on the other side of the world, and instead he'd been thrown into a situation completely out of his control. A situation where the lives of so many were depending on him to make the right decisions. He needed a new perspective. Needed his father's help. Needed a way to protect this town.

But how could he protect the town when he didn't even know who the enemy was?

He stared across the street at Morgan's house. He hadn't intended on making any ties here. He'd planned to come back and figure out his next step. Staying in Shadow Ridge had never been an option. What was it about her that seemed to wrap around his heart and bring healing? Her smile? Her laugh? It didn't matter. That was a place he couldn't go to. He'd failed, and he was so afraid that he was going to fail again.

He pulled his compass from his pocket.

If you ever lose your way. . .

He'd told Noah the truth when he said he never lost his way. Not physically anyway. But the darkness inside of him had made it impossible to find his way back to the light. Praying and sitting on a church pew had done nothing. Instead, he'd focused on routine and order. He found riding through the streets of town and checking on residents therapeutic. Something that fueled him for another day. A set time to get up. A set order of things to accomplish every day. It kept him focused and busy. But no matter how busy he stayed, there was still too much time to think.

The first rays of sun had just emerged across the horizon when a knock on the car window jolted him awake.

"Morning." Hope opened the driver's seat door then handed him a travel mug. "Thought you might want something hot."

"Ah," Jace said, taking a sip of the roasted chicory root drink. "Starbucks."

Hope laughed. "You didn't go home last night, did you?"

Jace shrugged and took another sip. "I guess I slept some."

"In this car?"

"I was worried about you, and it seemed like the coziest solution." He moved his neck in

a slow circle, trying to work out the kinks. "And it's not as if Mr. Lee has any plans to use it."

"That's what I love about you," Hope said, skirting around the car before slipping into the passenger seat beside him. "You care, really care for family and for this town. And Morgan."

Jace shifted his focus to his drink, trying to find a way to change the subject.

"Morgan and I stayed up talking last night," Hope continued.

"That's what I was afraid of."

"Why?" Hope held her mug in her hands and caught his gaze. "You told me it was just dinner."

"Maybe there was more to it."

"Like you kissed her?"

"If I remember correctly, she kissed me."

Hope smiled. "I don't think that's her version."

"Then let's just say it was mutual. Very mutual. Or at least I thought it was."

"So what's the problem?"

"I'm not sure. Just something I saw in her eyes afterward. She was about to say something when Gideon showed up. Something about things not working between us."

"And you're worried she's having second thoughts," Hope said. "Or maybe you're having second thoughts."

"Morgan's lost a lot." Jace took another sip, wishing he could stop the rising guilt. "And I never should have pushed."

Hope shifted in her seat and faced him. "I might be sticking my nose into the wrong place, but I think whatever she told you—whatever she implied—was coming from her head and not her heart."

"Don't try to fix this, Hope." He leaned against the headrest. "We're all feeling vulnerable right now. I won't take advantage of that with her."

"I just see how she lights up when you're in the room. And Noah adores you."

"I don't know."

"I do. But I also think you're afraid it's too good to be true."

He set the mug down on his thigh. "What do you mean?"

"We've *all* lost a lot this past year, Jace. You should be back in Atlanta, I should be married, and Morgan. . . Morgan lost her husband. It's not easy to get past that pain and love again."

"No, it's not." He tapped his hand on the steering wheel. "How are *you*, Hope?"

His sister shrugged. "The hardest thing is not knowing what happened to Chase. I imagine all sorts of awful things. He was escorting prisoners. There's no way to know if he's dead or alive."

Jace swirled his drink. "I'm sorry to dredge things up for you again."

"It's okay. I'm learning that life goes on and I have to find a way forward. So does Morgan. Just give her time. Something tells me it's going to be impossible for her to not to come around to your charms."

"Very funny."

"You need to go talk to her."

Jace glanced at his watch. "I know, but the sun's almost up, and I've got a bunch of men arriving any minute at the station to search for Frank."

"Don't put it off, Jace."

"I won't. I promise."

"Are you going out with the men?" she asked.

"No. I think it's better if I stay in town. I can't have another explosion go off while I'm not here."

"Stop worrying about things you can't control," Hope said, squeezing his hand. "You can't watch over us twenty-four seven. And that's okay. Now go do your job."

He squeezed her hand back. "Thanks for the drink."

"Take it with you. You can return the mug to Morgan when you come and talk to her."

Several of the men who had been a part of the search the day before were already sitting in the station lobby and chatting when Jace arrived.

"I need your help with a situation." Levi said, signaling Jace to the back office.

"Give me a minute, fellows." Jace stepped inside, then stopped at the sound of someone belting out Frank Sinatra's "My Way." "What's going on?"

"It's Charlie Rand. Helen locked him out of the house again."

"Is that who's singing?"

Levi nodded. "I put him in one of the cells because, as you might have guessed, he's drunk as a skunk."

Jace frowned. Another domestic fight and a drunk belting out songs from the big band era wasn't what he needed right now.

"We'll leave him in there for now, and hopefully he'll sleep it off." Jace started to turn back to the lobby, then stopped. "Where did that wheelbarrow come from?"

"It's Charlie's, complete with leather tobacco pouches and Mason jars filled with moonshine."

Jace picked up one of the pouches and smelled it. It was the same blend as the tobacco he'd found at the warehouse and in Frank's barn. "Where did he get all of this?"

"I'm not sure. I didn't get very far with him."

"Get the men ready to go out, but give me five minutes."

"Copy that, but what are you going to do?"

Jace spun around and headed toward the holding cells. "I need to talk with Charlie."

Shadow Ridge boasted three cells in the back of the station that had been mostly used for drunks and petty crimes over the past few months. Jace stopped in front of the first cell where Charlie lay on his back on the bed, still singing.

"Where did you get the moonshine and tobacco, Charlie?"

The man stopped singing and looked up. "What?"

"I said, where did you get the moonshine and tobacco?"

Charlie frowned. "I didn't steal it, if that's what you're thinking. I might be a drunk, but I'm not a thief. It's my own brew. I trade it."

"To who?"

"Lots of people."

"Have you ever sold to this man?" Jace held up Ricky's photo.

"Never seen him."

"Look again. Have you ever sold to this man?" Jace asked, still holding up the photo.

Charlie rubbed his unshaved jawline, then shook his head.

Jace showed him the sketch Tess had drawn the night before of the man with whom Owen had exchanged survival goods for medicine. "What about this man?"

Charlie looked away.

"Charlie. . ."

"Fine. I recognize him."

"What's his name?"

"Parker something."

"Parker what?"

"I have no idea." This time Charlie looked up and caught Jace's gaze. "It's not like we exchange LinkedIn information before we do a transaction."

"Okay." Jace didn't even try to mask his irritation. "Is he from around here?"

"If he is, I don't know him. I think he's some kind of middleman who travels from town to town."

"What does he give you for the moonshine?"

"Sometimes food. Sometimes grain or corn so I can make more moonshine."

"Jace." Levi stepped through the doorway. "I'm still waiting on two of the men, but there are a couple college kids here,

Carter and Adrian. You'll probably recognize them from town. They said it's urgent they speak with you."

Jace slapped his palms against his thighs. "It never ends, does it?"

"I told you everything I know," Charlie shouted. "Can I leave now?"

Jace ignored the question, then headed back into the lobby where the boys were waiting for him. Both wore swim trunks and T-shirts and looked like they'd just come from a frat party.

"What's going on, boys?" Jace set his hands on his hips.

"Yeah, well, we went up to Judson Springs yesterday. Thought we would camp out and do some swimming." Adrian glanced at Carter. "We'd found a couple scuba dive lights that still worked and wanted to try them out. See if we could find anything interesting down there."

"Did you?" Jace asked, still unsure what the point of their visit was.

"Yeah. We found a body."

CHAPTER FIFTEEN

JACE LEANED against the desk and studied the two boys standing in front of him. Tracking down another dead body had not been on his agenda today, but then again, had anything gone as planned recently? He searched for signs that they'd been drinking or smoking. The last thing he had time for today was a wild goose chase, but if they were telling the truth. . .

"How much did the two of you drink last night?" he asked.

"Oh, there was no drinking," Carter said, shaking his head. "Not when we're out swimming."

"So no moonshine or white lightning or whatever you want to call it?" Jace pressed.

Adrian's gaze dropped.

"This isn't a joke," Jace said, raising his voice. "I don't have time to spend my day looking for a non-existent body because you boys got spooked last night and saw a ghost."

"Fine." Adrian slid his hands into his back pockets. "We might have had a couple of drinks, but I promise. We weren't drunk, and we really did see a body."

Jace braced his hands against the desk, trying to compose his thoughts. The possibility of two dead bodies in twenty-four hours and a killer on the loose meant he'd better find out what was going on before someone else died.

"Do you know who it was?" Jace asked.

"We don't know because we never saw his face. His legs were tangled up in a rope and weighed down with. . ." Carter looked at Adrian. "I'm not sure what it was. Something like a brick or a cement block."

"But it was definitely a man," Levi said.

Adrian nodded. "Yes. Definitely a man."

"Can you tell me exactly where he was?" Jace asked.

"On the south side of the spring. Fifteen, maybe twenty feet down. There are a lot of rocks, but the water's pretty clear and with the lights, everything was illuminated. One of us could go with you, but it would be hard to miss him if you knew where to look."

"Did you see anything that might have pointed to how he was killed?" Jace asked.

"We didn't exactly stay around to find out."

"Do either of you have scuba gear?"

"Nah. We don't dive. Not with gear anyway."

"Okay." Jace signaled Levi to come with him. "I want you both to wait here. We'll be right back."

Jace could hear the men from the search team talking in the lobby as he stepped into the hall with Levi.

"What do you want to do?" Levi asked.

"I don't think we can wait to go search for the body," Jace said, still formulating his plan, "but we also need to send out the search team and find Frank if there's going to be any chance of capturing him."

"Pulling up a body could be complicated."

"I know." Jace nodded. "Especially if it's been anchored with something."

"You dive," Levi said.

"Yes, but I don't have any of my equipment here."

"Morgan and Tommy used to dive. In fact, if I remember correctly, she worked her way through college as an instructor. She'll likely have equipment." Levi rested his hands on his belt. "I might not dive, but I do know you shouldn't go down there alone."

Jace brushed away the suggestion. "I can't ask her to go diving for a dead body with me."

"Then come up with another option because you're going to need someone, Jace."

"Fine." Jace pushed away his lingering reservations. "I'll talk to her then head up to the springs. In the meantime, I want you to have the men reorganize the search area to a grid closer to the spring. Just in case this is connected, Frank wouldn't have anticipated our finding the body this fast. There are a number of cabins scattered throughout the area, with the majority of them empty."

"A perfect place to hide," Levi agreed, "but that area is still vast."

"If we don't find Frank today, I'll call off the search, but something tells me he isn't going to go too far. Not with his family still here."

The men helping him were already spread out thin. He was just going to have to go with the *least worst* option.

"Do you want me to go with them?" Levi asked.

"No," Jace said, thankful, not for the first time, that his brother was here. "I know resources are in short supply, but I want you to stay in town. We need a presence with all that's been going on, and an assurance of continued security at the bank."

"I'll get the team off, then start patrolling."

Jace stepped back into his office where Carter and Adrian were waiting, while Levi grabbed his pack and went to finish organizing the search. "Do either of you boys have a horse? I'll need one of you to come with me and show me exactly where you found the body."

"Mine's out front," Adrian said, standing up. "Carter needs to head home, but I'll come as long as you don't expect me to get in the water again. It's going to take me a long time before I can swim there again."

"Not a problem," Jace said, grabbing his hat. "Let's go."

THE WIND HAD PICKED up by the time they headed out of town with scuba gear and a body bag. Jace was surprised Morgan agreed to help him. It wasn't every day that he had to ask a civilian to search for a dead body. He rode between Morgan and Adrian, determined not to let his feelings distract him.

Not today.

Three miles north of town was a spring-fed pool, a stunning oasis in the middle of the cactus, grasslands, and rocks. When he was growing up, it had been one of his favorite places to spend a hot summer day. The water was not only warm, but full of fish. It had been the perfect getaway to a very different world. Some things hadn't changed. Kids and families in town still loved coming up here as they searched for some semblance of normal.

"Thank you for coming with me," he said to Morgan, wishing they were alone and that he could tell her what was really on his mind. That he was sorry about last night and the kiss that had somehow thrown off the balance of their friendship.

"You might have to hold your thanks until this is over," Morgan said. "I've logged a lot of hours diving, but it was always to see the marine life and to get that feeling like you're flying."

"Are you sure you're okay about this?"

"Okay about dragging up a dead body?" She tugged on the brim of her black, wide-brimmed cowboy hat to block the sun. "It's not the first thing I've had to do outside my comfort zone, and I'm sure it won't be the last."

He stole another glance at her. He'd seen her strength and could imagine her living out here a hundred-plus years ago in the Wild West. He knew it hadn't been easy, but she'd still managed to adapt to finding ways to make a life for her son.

"You think Keaton is the victim?" she asked, breaking into his thoughts.

"It's a logical assumption. Frank could have headed this direction, dumped Keaton's body, then planned to vanish."

"Keaton and Frank aren't the first people to disappear from Shadow Ridge."

"I know."

The wall of names on Main Street proved it.

Grasslands and cottonwoods surrounded them as they approached Judson Springs. Jace looked around at the trash scattered across the ground from a string of parties. Whoever had dumped the body had chosen the wrong location, never imagining how quickly it was going to be discovered.

Adrian pulled off his shoes, then scurried down toward the water. "This is where we dove in. Just past this inlet. It gets deep pretty fast."

"You're sure this is it?" Jace asked, carrying a pair of fins and a mask.

"Yeah. There are quite a few large rocks when you get past about fifteen feet, but he shouldn't be too hard to spot."

Jace put on his fins, then started toward the water. "Let me free dive first and see if I can locate the body, then we'll have a better idea of how we can get him to the surface."

"Are you sure?" Morgan asked, coming after him, carrying her diving equipment.

He turned back to her and read the concern in her eyes. "I'll be fine."

Before the Quake, a water body recovery would have been much more complex. Special body bags were typically used in order to keep forensic evidence intact, along with certain devices with a mechanical claw that could pull a body to the surface. Today, his goal was simple. He needed to be able to identify the body, and along with that, any clues that might lead to the killer.

Morgan handed him a diving light as he stepped into the water. He clipped it on his belt, put on his face mask, and after taking a deep breath, dove into the water.

MORGAN WATCHED as Jace disappeared into the spring. It had been at least a year since she'd last gone diving. She used to spend most of her free time in the water until she moved back to Shadow Ridge where diving trips had become fewer and farther between. Life had become busy with the restaurant, she'd gotten married, and Noah had come along, changing everything.

She pulled her hair back after taking off her hat, then pulled her equipment out of her bag so she was prepared to go down with Jace as soon as he located the body. Like Jace, Morgan had opted for shorts and a T-shirt instead of a dive suit for the warmer, spring-fed waters. With no dive shop in operation, she only had one usable cylinder, which meant Jace would have to breathe with the second regulator.

As she made her way closer to the shoreline, the cooler winds felt good on her back, and the sound of the water lapping against the rocks seemed inviting. The lonesome cry of a whip-poor-will nesting nearby nearly made her forget that this was a crime scene and they were searching for a body. Funny how she'd accused Jace of not taking any downtime because she was no different. On top of that, she spent way too much time worrying about what she couldn't control, and not near enough time enjoying what was around her.

Like a possible relationship with Jace.

She shoved away the thought as quickly as it had surfaced, still not ready to dissect those feelings. If someone had told her a year ago that she would be a widow searching for a dead body with a man she was starting to have feelings for, she would have thought they were crazy. And yet somehow it was true.

She studied the water where he'd gone down. She checked her watch. About forty-five seconds had passed.

"Everything okay?"

She looked back at Adrian sitting in the shade of a tree looking half asleep. "I hope so."

She went to the edge of the water. The gentle waves rippled toward the shore, but there was still no sign of Jace. After another ten seconds, he finally surfaced and gulped for air.

"Anything?" Morgan asked.

He shook his head, breathing heavily. "I'm going down again."

"Jace. . ."

"Yeah?"

She hesitated with her response. "Be careful."

He shot her a smile, took another deep breath, then dove down again. She was foolish to worry. And on top of that, she didn't need a man in her life. Just because life was hard didn't mean she couldn't make it alone.

But was it wrong to want someone to do life with?

Jace came back up for air a second time and took off his mask.

"What did you find?" she asked.

"The boys were right. The body's down about twenty feet I would guess. I could see him

with the light. Looks like a rope is wrapped around his legs and weighted down with several cement blocks." Jace shook the water out of his mask. "I'm going to have to cut the rope to get him out of there, which means we're ready for your scuba equipment."

She tried to shake the eerie tingling sensation that shot through her. "Okay. Do you have any idea yet who it is?"

"I wasn't able to see his face, but I do know he hasn't been down there long." He swam toward her and joined her on the shore. "You don't have to do this, Morgan. I can go down there alone."

"And what happens if you get into trouble?" she asked, grabbing her mask. "The first rule of diving is never go alone. There's no team up here with equipment for a water rescue, and I don't think Adrian is going to be much help." She glanced back at the sleeping figure. "I'm all you've got."

"Okay," he finally conceded. "And Morgan. . .thank you."

"You're welcome, but we need to hurry." She glanced at the sky. "It looks like this shift in the wind might be bringing a dust storm with it."

She handed him her second regulator, and they both waded out to the drop-off, swam to the right spot, and went under. Minnows gathered around her and a catfish swam by. On any other day she would have loved watching the fish swim around her. Today, all she could think about was a dead body.

She stayed beside Jace as they made their way to the bottom of the springs, taking long, slow breaths beside him. A few more feet down, Jace signaled to their left. She followed the direction of his hand, squeezing her eyes closed for a moment, not wanting to deal with the reality of what was in front of them.

Jace swam closer to the body and started sawing at the rope with his knife while she shifted her gaze away from the corpse, wishing not for the first time that she hadn't agreed to come. But this was not a time to be squeamish. She had a job to do.

The first rope broke loose, but the body still didn't move.

She looked at Jace who signaled "okay," checking that she was still good. She nodded and signaled back. Reassured, he went back to cutting the ropes. The body popped loose and rushed upward toward her.

Something brushed against her. Hair from the dead man. She kicked her legs, trying not to panic. Jace twisted his body around next to her, but the hand of the corpse had clamped onto his wrist. He jerked away from the body, losing his regulator in the process, then shot toward the surface as fast as he could.

Morgan reached the surface right behind him.

"Don't laugh," he said, ripping off his mask. "That corpse grabbed me."

She pulled off her own mask while treading water, her heart pounding. "I'm not going to laugh, but technically, he didn't grab you, you snagged him."

"Sounds like the same thing if you asked me." Jace shivered. "It takes a lot to throw me off, but I was face to face with that corpse. . . It was Keaton."

She nodded. "I know."

"Frank must have killed him and then dumped his body after he picked up the gear and weapons he demanded."

A chill sliced through her. "I know you didn't want to believe he was guilty."

Jace nodded, clearly affected by what they'd just found.

"You must have caught your shoulder on something. You're bleeding," she said, noticing the trail of blood running down his arm.

He looked down at the three-inch gash. "I didn't even feel it."

"It needs to be taken care of."

"I know, but our first priority is to get the body back to Shadow Ridge." He looked up, catching her gaze, and pointed to the water. "And we can keep *this* to ourselves."

Morgan pressed her lips together, unnerved at how Jace McQuaid had managed to make her want to smile in the middle of recovering a body. She pulled her mask back on and handed him the second regulator, then dove beside him back under the water.

CHAPTER SIXTEEN

THE RIDE back to Shadow Ridge felt like a scene from a horror movie. A wall of dust, triggered by the recent thunderstorms, darkened the skies above them and limited their visibility with its brown haze. With Adrian's reluctant help, they'd managed to get Keaton's body out of the water, into a body bag, and onto the back of Jace's horse.

Jace had dropped off the body for Hope to examine, then made sure Morgan got home safely before returning to the clinic. Hope ushered him into one of the exam rooms, but he wasn't interested in waiting for his sister to clean the cut on his shoulder. "My shoulder's fine. What I really need is some answers."

"Answers can wait," Hope said, pulling supplies from the overhead cupboard. "I need to make sure that cut doesn't get infected. Besides, I'm not a medical examiner. I don't have the equipment or knowledge to do a thorough autopsy."

"All I need is your best educated guess, Hope."

She told him to take off his shirt and sit on the exam table. "I'm out of numbing gel."

"I've been through far worse than this scratch."

"Here's what I know, from a very initial exam." Hope set down what she was going to need, then took a second look at his cut. "I dragged out one of my medical books while you were taking Morgan home. Keaton had froth in the upper and lower airways, which is a sign of drowning."

"So he wasn't dead when he went into the water."

Hope shook her head, then started cleaning the cut. "My initial theory is that he was hit on the back of the head, knocked unconscious, then dumped into the water."

"But he was murdered."

"That seems pretty certain, but I can't do any lab work that might give me evidence of who his murderer was. You're going to have to figure that out yourself."

Jace glanced at his shoulder as she started stitching it up. "I'm not sure I need lab results to know who killed him. The last time anyone saw Keaton, he was being held hostage by Frank. I guess I need to stop looking for another explanation."

"So Morgan went to the springs with you?" Hope asked.

Jace winced as she tugged the stitches together. "I needed her equipment, and she insisted she go with me as my dive partner."

"I just find it interesting that you kiss her one night and the next day ask her to go with you to find a dead body."

"The two situations had nothing to do with each other."

"I find that hard to believe. I'm pretty sure Morgan's not the only diver in town."

"You're reading too much into this, Hope."

"Maybe." She took a step back, then pulled off her gloves. "I'll put some ointment and a bandage on it, but try to keep it dry."

Jace jumped off the table. "Yes, ma'am."

"Did you talk to her?" Hope asked.

Jace started putting his shirt back on. "I didn't exactly have a chance. Not only was Adrian with us, I rode back with a dead body on my horse and a dust storm ripping through town. I don't know about you, but I didn't think it seemed like the right timing."

"Is it ever?"

He felt another wave of regret wash through him. That unnerving feeling that no matter what decisions he made, they were wrong. And the consequences couldn't be erased.

"I'm sorry." She stepped in front of him. "This is hitting you hard, isn't it?"

"I just hate the fact that I didn't stop this. That there's another man dead who shouldn't be."

Hope reached out and squeezed his uninjured shoulder. "You couldn't stop this, Jace. You've done an amazing job protecting this town, but there's only so much you can do. Keaton's death isn't your fault, and you can't lay that on yourself."

"Maybe. I don't know."

"It's been a long couple of days. Go home. Get something to eat and a good night's sleep. You'll feel better tomorrow."

An hour later, Jace rode toward the outskirts of town on Brisket. The dust storm had left behind a fiery painted sky of orange and yellow as the sun sank toward the horizon. The white silhouette of the old chapel built from rock and adobe stood in front of him. The structure had always been a place of peace in the midst of a world spinning into chaos. A place to come and pray or just find some solitude. But lately that peace and solitude had become impossible to find.

The search team had returned to the station about the same time he had, but they hadn't been able to pick up Frank's trail.

Which meant that they they'd made no progress in figuring out the truth today. Jace had sent them all home to their families, then decided he needed to clear his head.

He rode up to the church, then tied Brisket to the old hitching post before walking inside and sitting down on one of the wooden pews. He wasn't sure what he was searching for. Answers? Peace from the memories that kept him up at night? Lately, it felt as if there was nowhere to run.

The wooden door clicked open behind him, "Sorry, I was just locking up. Didn't know anyone was here."

Jace stood up. "Matthew. I can go. I was just needing to clear my head."

"No, Jace. Stay as long as you want. This is a good place to come for that, though God isn't limited to this building."

"Then why can't I find Him?" Jace hung his head, hating the admission.

"I know for me, I find that no matter where I go, God has been right there all along. I just wasn't looking in the right place, or have been unwilling to acknowledge His presence. Jesus was right when He said 'seek and you will find.'"

Jace mulled over the preacher's answer, but it seemed like the God who created the universe and set the world in motion wouldn't be interested in games of hide-and-seek. And how was he supposed to justify why God would allow so much loss around him? His father. . .Jeremiah's family. . .Hope. . .Morgan. . .and now Keaton's family. The list went on and on.

"Would you like some company?" Matthew asked.

"Company. Answers. I'm open to just about anything right now."

Matthew took off his ball cap and sat down on the pew in front of Jace. "How's your father?"

"Lost. Drifting. I've never seen him like this before. Never seen him give up on life. Physically, he's slowly getting better, but emotionally. . ."

"He lost a lot. The love of his life. His ability to do his job, which I know for Garrett McQuaid, was tied up in his identity and purpose. That kind of loss takes time to redeem, and grief itself has no timetable. Nor is it linear."

"It's just hard," Jace said, letting the pain seep through the cracks of his soul. "My father was always the one who helped me when I lost my direction. He'd remind me of the need to refocus on my heavenly Father, but now. . . I can't find that place again. That peace. I guess I thought if I came here. . . I don't know. I'm not even sure what I'm looking for."

"Proof that God is still here even though the world is falling apart around us."

Jace frowned. "That sounds like a lack of faith."

"God understands. I've found that He has a way of meeting us where we are and is far bigger than what we see."

Jace ran his hand across the worn grain of the pew, trying to wrap his mind around the truth in the statement. He believed, and yet he'd still found it so hard to apply his faith to his circumstances. He stared at the wooden cross hanging on the wall, the familiar sense of guilt wrapping around his heart. He'd gone to church his whole life. Memorized scriptures in Sunday school. Gone to youth meetings and prayer vigils. And then life happened. He'd seen the dark side of the world and human nature. The hatred in the killing. Things that he couldn't justify. If God really was out there somewhere, why didn't He sweep down and just end it? At least for the wicked. Instead there was so much suffering and hurt.

"What are you thinking?" Matthew asked.

"I haven't felt God's presence for a long time. I just feel so lost, and I'm not sure I can fight any longer. I don't know how to fix things. All I see is hurt and loss. . .I can't find God anymore."

"You've had to deal with a lot of hard stuff, Jace. Not just here in Shadow Ridge, holding this town together, but your time in the military as well."

Jace worked to push aside the memories. "I've tried searching for Him. Tried to find that voice that used to speak to me. But there's only silence. Like the desert at night, it just seems to go on and on. No answers. I don't how to get myself back there again."

"Maybe you're searching in the wrong places. I think you've fallen into the trap that too

many people have. Too often we turn to man, or things, or even our own abilities for the answers instead of God. We don't stop and listen. We get caught up in religion and not the power of His presence." Matthew leaned forward. "You went to war. You know what it's like to stand and feel the enemy surrounding you. This is no different. It's a spiritual battle, son. We can't forget that. What brought you here tonight?"

"I don't know." Jace hesitated. "Morgan asked me if I thought God was responsible for what's happening. What frustrates me is I know the right answers, but I don't know if I believe them anymore. And to be honest, that scares me."

"I'll be honest, you're not the only one who's faith has been stretched through of all this, but it's a good thing."

Jace let out a low chuckle. "That's pretty hard to see right now."

"Agreed, but think about it this way. God can use bad events for His glory, but that doesn't mean He's behind them."

"He could have stopped this."

"Yes. In His sovereign power He could. But there are numerous stories in the Bible where things happened that were not God's will—"

"Because God allows us free will."

Matthew nodded. "God put inside us a hunger for Him. Hunger for His presence. Something that can only be filled by Him. With all that's happened this past year, your direction might have changed, but that truth hasn't changed. God is still sovereign. *And* He can and will use this situation for His purposes. He can transform Satan's purposes into His."

"That's why I rode out here tonight. I thought I'd come here, spend some time out in the desert, and try to find the answers."

"But truthfully, the answers aren't out there, Jace. In many ways, you're like your father. You'd lost your purpose, and coming back to Shadow Ridge put you on a trajectory you never could have imagined. And yet at the same time. . .you weren't going back to the military, were you?"

Jace glanced up at the man of God and frowned. "I've only told one person about leaving the military. I planned to tell my parents after their anniversary party, but then. . .then everything changed, and suddenly it didn't matter anymore."

"I've become pretty good at reading people while trying to listen to the Holy Spirit speak to me," Matthew said, breaking the moment of silence between them. "Not just their physical injuries, but their hearts as well. And I know you didn't come back to Shadow Ridge to take over for your father, but I believe God brought you back to this town for a reason. This town needs you, but you also need this town. And you need more help doing what you do. If you don't get it, you won't make it."

Morgan had pretty much said the same thing. But even she didn't know that he'd finished his last military contract and walked away without looking back, determined to move forward in something completely different. But then the Quake had shaken all of his plans.

"What am I supposed to do?" Jace said finally. "I feel as if I don't have the strength to keep doing this. I'm supposed to get up every morning, seven days a week, and make sure this town survives. At least in the military, we knew who the enemy was, and we could plan and strategize accordingly. But I don't even know who we're fighting. I don't know if the Chinese or the Russians have taken over the country. I don't know who just killed two of my people, or who's stealing our food. I don't know if all of this will be over tomorrow, or in a week, or in ten years. How am I supposed to save this town?"

"Is that what you think God is asking you to do?" Matthew asked.

"Isn't it?"

"Maybe, but saving an entire town. . .that's a pretty big burden on your shoulders." Matthew grasped the top of the wooden pew in front of them. "I've always loved this place. Do you know the history of this building?"

Jace looked up, surprised by the shift in the conversation.

"It was built in the late 1800s by my great-great-grandfather," Matthew continued, "along with a few other men. They worked hard every day just to survive. Food had to be hunted or caught, and crops planted. Travel was dangerous and difficult because of bandits and thieves on the roads, and any rest or recreation was hard to come by."

Jace couldn't help but chuckle. "Sounds a bit like today."

"Exactly. We might think that everything going on now has never happened before, but there really is nothing new under the sun. Can I give you some unsolicited advice?"

Jace looked up and caught the pastor's gaze. "Always."

"Do you remember in the Bible when Moses was serving as judge for the Israelites? He worked from morning to evening, settling disputes, and basically trying to save them."

"I think I do."

"Do you remember what Moses' father-in-law said to him?"

Jace shook his head.

"He told him to share the load with other capable men."

Jace let out a sharp huff of air. "I have a few working under me, but it isn't like I can pay them. And most of them are just family men trying to survive. How can I expect them to help secure the town on a regular basis when they're already so busy?"

"You can't keep this pace up. No one can. You need help, and that's okay."

"It seems more like a failure in my book."

"Think of how many people in the Bible considered themselves failures, and yet God used them. Moses was called by God, and he felt inadequate. Remember his conversation with God in front of the burning bush? David, Peter, Esther. . . God used all of them, despite their being unprepared and unqualified." Matthew shifted in the pew and laid his arm along the back. "When is the last time you took a day off, or even just a couple hours to go fishing?"

Jace tried to stuff the nightmares back into their box. "I don't exactly have time. There's always something to do. Some kind of need. And if I stop—"

"The world might shut down?"

Jace looked up. "I think it already did that."

"Exactly. And yet life goes on."

"You don't understand." Jace closed his eyes. He could see the flash of the bomb and smell the burning flesh and hear the screams. "This isn't the first time I've failed."

"So this is all about making up for past sins?"

"Maybe." Jace stood as the pastor's words pierced through him. "But you don't need to hear my problems. I'm sure you have to deal with enough of that every day."

"I *could* use your help with one thing."

"Of course."

"I've been convicted that the church here needs to step up and work more with the community. Not just programs, but life on life. As you know, there are a lot of people hurting. As our law enforcement in town, I've wanted to connect with you and brainstorm about how that might work."

"I would definitely be interested."

"Good. And in the meantime, give yourself some grace. If you need something. . .anything. . .you know where to find me."

Jace slipped out the back of the church, feeling a shift in his thinking. But he couldn't dwell on Matthew's words right now. He had to catch the killer.

CHAPTER SEVENTEEN

JACE HEADED BACK toward the police station after his morning rounds just as the sun was cresting the horizon. He'd always loved this time of day, when the early morning light spilled colors over a desert filled with more scrub and cactus than houses or telephone poles. The sky itself seemed to go on forever in a terrain filled with vast deserts and rugged mountains that were covered with pine and aspen. This place brought with it a welcome solitude he'd sometimes found himself craving after leaving Shadow Ridge.

He'd had little time to appreciate the beauty around him since his return. Instead, every day had been focused on saving the town he'd said he'd never come back to. Despite its beauty, this place was too isolated and inaccessible. He'd left years ago with high hopes of saving the world, something you couldn't do in Shadow Ridge.

Wind swirled around him, blowing a couple of tumbleweeds across the road. He'd enjoyed coming back for Christmas and other family events with his siblings, but there had been nothing pulling him to stay.

Not until Morgan.

His jaw tensed. He hadn't planned to fall for her, but did it really matter? Once the grid was up again, he'd have the option to stay or go, and he'd never questioned his plan to leave Shadow Ridge.

To do what?

The thought took him by surprise. Leaving had never been in question, even though he wasn't sure what he was going back to. His father was wrong. He wasn't cut out to do this kind of work anymore. Besides, despite what Matthew had said to him, how could a broken person like him fix this? He had access to limited resources, and what he had was stretched thin. This wasn't something he was going to be able to do indefinitely.

Or was it?

God put inside us a hunger for Him. . . I believe God brought you back to this town for a reason.

Matthew's words surfaced, but this time he didn't fight the counsel.

He'd been running for a long time. Looking for something that only God could fill. Was that the problem? What if God had brought him here not as some kind of punishment, but to help him find his purpose? To find who he was in Him.

Dust billowed ahead. Someone was coming toward him fast on horseback. He reached for his weapon but then recognized his brother.

Jace pulled on the reins and brought Brisket to a stop, his thoughts on hold for the moment. "What's going on?"

"I came out to look for you. The sheriff from Van Horn is here with three other men. They were ambushed, and one of them was shot."

"They're at the clinic?" Jace asked.

Levi nodded. "I gave the sheriff a quick briefing about what has happened here then came to find you."

"Let's go."

Five minutes later, Jace stepped into the clinic in front of his brother. He headed through the busy lobby straight for the back where Hope was scrubbing her hands under a pitcher of water with one of her nurses.

"I can't talk right now, Jace."

"Just tell me what's going on?"

"I have a patient with a gunshot wound. I'm about to do an emergency surgery."

A man with a sheriff's badge and a Stetson hat walked up to him. "Jace McQuaid. It's good to see you again. It's been a long time."

Jace nodded. In nine months, this was only the second time the law man had managed to visit their town.

"Sheriff Estrada. You and I need to talk."

"Go ahead," Hope said to her brother. "There's nothing you can do here."

"Come get us when you're done," Jace said.

Hope nodded. "Of course."

"We can go to my office," Jace said, making a quick one eighty. "Are you hungry?"

"Starved." The sheriff grabbed his leather pack and followed Jace to the police station.

At the office, Jace gave instructions for Levi to arrange food for the men. He poured a glass of water from the water dispenser in his office and handed it to the sheriff.

The sheriff downed it quickly, then held out his glass again. "I'll take anything wet at this point. It's dry out there, and we're running low on supplies."

"We'll get you and your men resupplied with anything you need," Jace said, motioning for the man to sit down in the cracked leather chair. "It's been a long time since we've seen you."

"I know, and I'm sorry. But as you know, it's a bit like the wild west out there." Sheriff Estrada finished the second glass, then sat down. "How far have you gone out?"

Jace leaned back against his desk. He had a dozen questions of his own, but for the moment he was going to simply follow the lawman's lead.

"I've had men go as far as Fort Stockton," Jace said, "but with the uptick in bandits and lawlessness, I've been leery of sending my men out or my being gone too long. A couple of the men convinced me to let them do a week-long trip recently and bring back as much information as they could. They were planning to go all the way to Midland, but they're late."

Sheriff Estrada stretched his legs out in front of him. "I'm not surprised."

"What's going on out there?" Jace asked.

"I've been visiting as many towns as I can. In some, people have come together. They're growing food and implementing specific protocols that will help get them through the winter. Others don't have any rule of law, some have been taken over by gangs, and some towns are just. . .gone."

Jace rubbed the back of his neck, the confirmation of his fears alarming. "My brother said you were ambushed."

Sheriff Estrada nodded. "About four miles outside of Shadow Ridge. I got a good look at only one of them, and I know we hit at least one of theirs."

"We could put a posse together and go look for them," Jace said.

Levi walked in with a bowl of beans and a large slice of pan de compo and handed it to the sheriff. The sheriff dug into the food then closed his eyes for a moment.

"You don't know how good this tastes," he said before taking another bite. "Reminds me of my grandmother. She used to make the best beans in a cast-iron pot on her woodstove."

"We have several women who sell breakfast most mornings," Levi said. "I could get you some chicory coffee as well, if you'd like. I've just fed your men."

"I appreciate it, and yes, I would love some chicory coffee. Thank you." The sheriff turned back to Jace as Levi left to get the drink. "So what does something like this cost you?"

"The women will take just about anything. Sugar, spices, salt, produce, candles. . ."

The sheriff broke off a piece of the bread and sopped up some of the juice from his beans. "It's an adjustment, isn't it?"

"Without a doubt."

"Listen." The sheriff set his spoon down. "Back to your suggestion about putting together a posse. Do you have men who have enough experience to take on this gang?"

"I think so. In fact, we've just been tracking two of our men."

"You didn't find them?"

"We found one of them." Jace hesitated. "Someone dumped him in Judson Springs."

"And your brother said another man had been murdered at the warehouse."

Jace nodded.

"I'm sorry." The sheriff held up his glass and motioned for more water. "Do you mind?"

Jace filled the glass again, then handed it back to the older man. "Do you know who's behind this?"

"There's a group of eight men who have been attacking isolated towns and then selling the goods on the black market. That's who we believe we ran into. They're called the Buffalo Riders because they leave behind Buffalo nickels at places they rob. They also have vehicles and a supply of stolen fuel."

"Hold on." Jace skirted around his desk, then pulled the coin he'd found at the bank out of a drawer and held it up. "Like one of these?"

"Exactly. Where did you find it?"

"This one was left after an attack on our bank. Our warehouse was also robbed a couple days ago, though I didn't find one of these there."

"Now that you know what you're looking for, I wouldn't be surprised if you find one there as well." Sheriff Estrada set his empty bowl down on the desk, then sat back. "Though I find it odd that they would hit a bank. From what I know, they never steal money."

"They weren't after money," Jace said. He explained about the emergency supplies the bank manager had stored there.

"But how did they know what was in there?" the sheriff asked. "Unless it was an inside job?"

"We don't know yet. Have you been able to ID any of the men?"

"We have some sketches, thanks to a handful of witnesses." The sheriff grabbed his leather pack next to him and pulled out a folder. "We still need to ID them."

Jace waited for the sheriff to lay the drawings on the desk, then stepped in front of them, slowly working through the details of each person. "Hang on. We might have something."

Jace went around to the front of his desk, retrieved the sketches Tess had made from the drawer, and laid them next to the sheriff's sketches.

"Looks like you have your own artist," the sheriff said, folding his arms across his chest. "I have to say, they're better than mine."

"It's my sister. She's been a huge help." Jace lined up two of the drawings. "These have got to be the same man."

"Agreed."

"And this one. . ." Jace tapped one of the sketches. "I'm pretty sure I can ID this one."

"Who is he?"

"Ricky Addison," Jace said, not surprised by the connection. "His sister-in-law lives here."

"What's her name?"

"Morgan Addison."

The sheriff looked up at him. "That name sounds familiar."

"She owned the diner down the road. Her grandmother was from Mexico and made some of the best enchiladas you've ever tasted."

"That's it." The sheriff nodded. "I've eaten at that diner dozens of times, and you're right. I've had the enchiladas, but she also had some of the best pie. Could do with a big slice right now, actually." He glanced at his empty bowl of beans. "But that doesn't make her innocent."

Jace's jaw tensed. "She's not involved with her brother-in-law, I can promise you that."

"So you know her?"

"She's a friend," Jace said.

The sheriff jumped on the connection. "From what I've heard about the warehouse robbery and the bank, there's likely an insider connection to someone, or maybe *someones* in town. I heard that one of your men is a suspect behind two murders."

"That's true," Jace said, not sure where the man was headed.

"What do you know about Addison's sister-in-law?"

"She's a recent widow and now a single mom," Jace said. "And I know for a fact she hasn't had contact with him. In fact, she came to me when she thought she saw him in town near the blast sight. Told me that if it was him, he was up to no good, but that she hadn't spoken to him for over a year."

"Even if you're right, I'm going to need to talk with her."

"All right, though there is someone else we also need to talk to."

"Who's that?"

"The bank manager implied a possible relationship between Ricky and one of the tellers."

"Bring her in, then. Both women." The sheriff rubbed his beard. "I'd also like to see your notes on the crime scenes."

"No problem. We have both photos and sketches." Jace frowned, hoping the man had a softer side to him when he spoke with Morgan. "I'll have my brother go get her while I get you what we have."

"I appreciate it. The sooner we can get this gang sent off to the salt mines, the better."

Jace hesitated in the doorway. "The salt mines?"

"I have word from a reliable source that criminals are doing hard labor in salt mines, coal mines, and other industry mines across the state. Makes sense to me, with no functioning prisons."

"What else have your sources told you ?" Jace asked.

"If you mean what took the grid down, I probably don't know any more than you do. It's still a mystery; though once we get this gang behind bars, I've been tied down to this area, but I'm planning to try to make it to Dallas in one piece. Going to see if I can get some answers."

Jace headed to find his brother, feeling as if he'd just stepped back in time two hundred years. Using prisoners as enslaved laborers might sound good, but he knew that with conditions as they were, using forced labor was the only way most industries could turn a profit. How long would it take for demand to outrun supply and for corruption in law enforcement to run rampant?

Twenty minutes later, Morgan stepped into Jace's office with a guarded look on her face, making him wonder if he should have spoken with her first. He had no idea how the sheriff was going to handle the interview.

"Mrs. Addison," Sheriff Estrada said, setting down the files he'd been looking at. "Thank you for coming."

"Please," she said, shaking his hand. "You can call me Morgan."

The sheriff leaned back against the desk while Jace took a seat across from Morgan. "I understand that Ricky Addison is your brother-in-law."

"He is."

Estrada held up the sketch his artist had composed. "We believe he's been involved with a gang that's committed a number of burglaries across the county. And in comparing notes with Jace, we have reason to believe that the gang had inside information in a number of towns, including this one."

Morgan studied the photo. "It definitely could be him."

"When is the last time you saw your brother-in-law?"

"Last year, before the grid went down. He came for my husband's birthday."

The sheriff folded his arms across his chest. "What was he doing for a living at that time?"

"He said he had a job up in Washington state and was heading up there. Something in the fishing industry. He needed money for transport, which was probably the real reason for his visit."

"Any felonies or run-ins with the law?"

"He'd been arrested a couple of times."

"We know he's been in the area for the past few weeks." The sheriff stood up and started pacing. "I find it hard to believe he hasn't come to see you."

Morgan glanced at Jace before turning back to the sheriff. "I already told Jace I think I might have seen him in town two days ago, but we were never close, and his brother is dead. Even if he is here, he'd have no reason to see me."

"I don't know." The sheriff pulled off his glasses and cleaned them on the bottom of his shirt before putting them back on. "Makes perfect sense to me that he would want to check on his brother's widow. Especially if he was looking for inside information. You would be his perfect inroad to Shadow Ridge."

"Like I said. . ." Morgan's frown deepened. "We weren't close."

"We have compelling evidence that your brother-in-law is involved not only in the murder of the man in your warehouse, but also in the shooting of one of my men. We don't know if he's going to make it or not. Anyone involved in harboring the man who pulled the trigger on my deputy is just as guilty as he is."

"Wait a minute." Morgan's jaw dropped. "Are you accusing me of being involved in all of this?"

"I've already told you that I can personally vouch for Morgan—"

"So I'm assuming you spend a lot of time with her," the sheriff said, interrupting Jace. "You know who comes and goes from her house twenty-four seven?"

"No, but I—"

"It's my job to investigate and ask the hard questions, McQuaid, not just take someone's word for it. And I don't have time to pussyfoot around so I don't hurt people's feelings. I have to shake the truth out of people, or I'll never get anything."

"Agreed, but I'm not the only one who can vouch for Morgan," Jace said, feeling his irritation rise. "Ask anyone in Shadow Ridge. She'd never betray this town."

"Thank you, but I don't need you to defend me," Morgan said, now seemingly angry at both of them. "Is there anything else you need from me, Sheriff? I need to go get my son."

"Not at present, but I'll be in touch. And if your brother in-law does happen to show up, I will expect you to notify the authorities immediately."

"Of course."

"I'll walk you out," Jace said.

She hurried ahead of him, ignoring the offer. But he wasn't going to leave things like this between them.

"Morgan—"

She turned around to face him once she was outside on the street, her hands fisted on her hips. "You could have warned me that the man was going to blindside me. Accusing me of harboring a fugitive? Really? I came to you about Ricky. I'm not hiding anything."

"I know, and I'm sorry. I had no idea he was going to accuse you of lying. I told him you hadn't seen Ricky and that there was no way you were involved."

Her hands relaxed at her sides. "You seem to be doing a whole lot of apologizing lately."

"I really am sorry."

"It doesn't matter." She shook her head. "I don't have the time or energy to argue."

Jace frowned as she turned away, feeling he couldn't win no matter what he did. "Morgan. You need to understand—"

She spun back around, her face flushed. "No, you need to understand. I know your heart is in the right place, but my only priority right now is to protect my son. I never should have kissed you, Jace McQuaid. I don't need you to protect me, and I don't need you in my life."

"Morgan—"

Her words stung as she walked away. He knew she'd lost a lot. Understood that she had a son to protect. But why did she have to be so self-reliant?

The sheriff looked up when he came back inside. "Are you ready to go?"

"Yes. But I would appreciate it if you wouldn't come in here accusing people in my town without evidence."

Estrada waved his hand dismissively. "I have a job to do, and I don't have time to play nice. I need to find these men before someone else gets hurt. Even if it means hurting people's feelings."

"I understand, but I need you to trust me and my instincts as well. It'll save us both time." Jace opened the locked cabinet on the back wall of the office, not waiting for the man to respond. "We've got flashlights, limited solar chargers for radios, and flares we can use. I'm going to put my brother in charge of organizing the posse, but before we head out. . ." Jace set one of the packs on the desk. "I need to take care of something."

CHAPTER EIGHTEEN

MORGAN WALKED down the aisle of one of the greenhouses, pleased with how the tomatoes were growing. Tommy had always been the one with the green thumb, and had always teased her that while she might make the best enchiladas *verdes* he'd ever tasted, she couldn't grow a plastic plant. Turned out, when Tommy died, she'd been forced to take over the running of the greenhouses, and had discovered she had a knack for learning. The greenhouses had been built behind the house on their large plot of land, and currently produced tomatoes, bell peppers, and cucumbers. The small team who had worked with Tommy had stayed on, finding feasible ways to adapt the running of the greenhouses without electricity. They took what they needed for each of their families, donated a portion to the church's food bank, then traded the excess produce for other foods and items.

Morgan walked down a row of tomatoes, checking for symptoms of mold. She stopped halfway down to pull off a Mini San Marzano tomato. Her mouth watered as she bit into it, bringing a smile to her lips. Thanks to Miguel, her manager, some of the old-timers, and hives of bumblebees for pollination, they'd managed to produce a crop that was going to help keep food on the table year-round. She'd already started canning tomatoes and salsa, and pickling cucumbers. Tommy would have been proud of her.

She glanced down at her wedding ring, shaken when her thoughts switched to Jace. She felt guilty over the way she'd left things with him. She knew he wanted more than just a friendship to develop between them. But no matter how much life had changed, she wasn't ready to fall in love again, and she had no plans of opening up her heart to someone just because she needed him. No. If she ever married again, it would be for love, not for convenience.

Then why had she kissed him?

She dropped her hands to her sides and breathed in the comforting, earthy scent of the greenhouse, trying to settle the anxiety inside her. The anxiety of moving on without Tommy. She started walking again. His picture still hung in the living room, their family pictures and snapshots on the refrigerator. She had no idea how to let go of that. How to push aside everything she'd known and start something new. Fear had continued to encroach its way around her heart, stopping her from letting anyone in. And once the lights came back on—if they ever did—she didn't want to regret the choices she'd made for herself and Noah.

Something clattered behind her.

She touched the handle of the holstered Glock at her side Jace had insisted she carry. "Noah?"

She headed toward the corner of the room to the small table where he'd been playing. A bird that had gotten caught in the greenhouse fluttered past her and landed on one of the wooden crossbeams. She blew out a sharp breath. She was letting her imagination get away with itself. Jace had suggested she get more security, so she'd hired two locals to guard her property at night after the workers went home. With all that was going on in town, she might need to hire more.

"Noah?"

Still no answer.

She turned the corner, then stopped. His backpack, the coloring page he'd been working on, and a couple of attempts at paper airplanes were on the table, but where was Noah? Her gut clenched. She'd warned him over and over not to wander off. She called him again. Still no answer. She headed toward the house. Noah was standing on the back porch, licking a lollipop and talking to two men.

A shot of adrenaline flooded through her gut as she recognized the figure. She ran toward the house, trying to settle her jumbled thoughts.

She'd been right about Ricky being in town. He had on the same red ball cap she'd seen him wearing in town, his hair was past his collar, and he'd grown a beard.

"Ricky."

She also knew she was right about him being up to no good.

"How do you like your surprise, Mom?" Noah asked, standing proudly next to his uncle. "It's Uncle Ricky. He brought me daddy's favorite candy."

"Vero Mangos." Ricky looped his thumbs through his belt loops. "I thought Noah might remember. And you, Morgan. . . You're looking prettier than I remember."

Morgan shifted her gaze from Noah to the other man, who was holding a duffel bag. To Noah, Ricky was a favorite uncle who came around every once in a while bringing candy and gifts. To her, he was a troublemaker who always came wanting something. The last time he'd managed to talk Tommy into enough cash for transport to where he promised him he had a job. But Ricky's presence only meant trouble.

"What do you want?" she asked.

"That's not the way to treat your favorite brother-in-law." Ricky's smile faded. "I heard about my brother's death and came to pay my respects. I can't believe he's gone. How are you doing?"

"It hasn't been easy, but we're doing okay."

"I apologize for the delay, but as you know, travel isn't what it used to be. My partner here and I are passing through town on business, but I also heard there was a break-in at the warehouse. Just wanted to make sure you're okay. Seems like these greenhouses might be a bit of a high-value target."

Morgan forced herself to maintain eye contact. "Seems to be an interesting coincidence that you're here right when the break-in happened."

"Nothing more than a coincidence, I'm sure." Ricky pulled Noah up against his leg. "Looks like you're doing pretty well here. You're one of the lucky ones. Already had greenhouses up and running before this fiasco struck. Looks like they're doing well."

"It's a lot of work, but we manage." Her jaw tensed. "Noah, I want you to go to your room so I can talk to your uncle."

Ricky touched the Colt at his hip. "Noah can stay."

Morgan caught the threatening tone in his voice, one she knew she couldn't just ignore. There was no telling what Ricky had done over the last few months. And while she'd always believed he wouldn't hurt them, he and his friend were here for more than a friendly chat.

"It's been too long since I've seen you, Noah," Ricky said. "How old are you now? Eleven? Twelve?"

Noah laughed. "I'm six."

"Ah, of course." Ricky's smile disappeared. "One of the reasons I'm here is because there are a few things of my brother's that he promised to give me from his gun collection."

"Tommy never told me that."

"It was something private between him and me."

Morgan pressed her shoulders back and raised her chin, trying to project a confidence she didn't have. "I'm going to need to ask you to leave, Ricky."

"Can't do that. Plus, I promised Noah here I have a new set of Legos for him out in my truck."

Noah's eyes widened. "You have a truck that works?"

"It will as long as I have fuel."

"Can I go get it with him, Mom?" Noah started jumping up and down. "Please?"

"Not today, Noah."

There was no way her son was going anywhere with this man. And no way she was going to give up her guns to him either.

"I was hoping you'd be a little bit more. . .cooperative." His fingers wrapped around the grip of his gun, upping her panic. "The last time Tommy showed them to me they were inside. Shouldn't take me long to pack them up, and I'll be out of your hair."

She struggled to rationalize her fear, not wanting to believe that Ricky's threats were more than a bluff. But something in Ricky's tone convinced her he wouldn't hesitate to use his nephew as a pawn if needed. He'd never had any sense of family. Clearly that hadn't changed over the past few months. She started for the house, trying to come up with a scenario that didn't have him walking out with any of her guns. Also one where Noah didn't get stuck in the crosshairs.

"Tommy sold several of his guns, and—"

"I know Tommy built a hidden closet, Morgan."

She hesitated, out of options for the moment. She walked slowly to the gun closet and opened the hidden door. Ricky's partner started shoving Tommy's hunting rifles and handguns into the bag. Her stomach cinched. Losing the guns didn't hurt as much as knowing that Tommy's brother would do this to her.

"Where's the rest of your ammunition?" Ricky asked.

Morgan held his gaze. "It's all in there."

"I don't believe that. I know my brother. He kept it separate in ammunition cans. I'm going to need you to show me."

"Why do you need all these?" Noah asked.

"Just borrowing them so my friends and I can go hunting. You like hunting for rabbits, don't you?"

Noah grinned. "Maybe I can go with you? I have a slingshot. And my mom can make the best rabbit stew you've ever had."

"Noah—" Morgan started.

"One last thing." Ricky took a step closer to Morgan. "Your wedding ring."

"Don't do this," Morgan said. "You know how much it means to me. Besides, it's not worth anything anymore."

"You'd be surprised what people will trade hoping that things get back to normal."

She glanced down at her hand and slowly slid off the ring Tommy had given her and handed it to him.

Ricky shoved the ring into his pocket, then tousled Noah's hair. "I'll bring you a rabbit, if I catch enough."

Someone knocked on the front door.

"Morgan?"

Morgan's breath caught at the sound of Jace's voice.

"It's Officer McQuaid!" Noah squealed.

Ricky grabbed Noah and put his hand over his mouth to silence him.

CHAPTER NINETEEN

JACE GLANCED in the open living room window, with blue curtains blowing in the breeze, but he couldn't see anyone. He knew someone was in the house. He'd heard voices as he came up the walk. But now it was quiet.

He knew she was mad, but ignoring him wasn't like her.

He knocked again. "Morgan, is everything okay?"

"Sorry, but I'm in the middle of something, Officer McQuaid."

Officer McQuaid?

His worry ratcheted up. Morgan had never called him Officer McQuaid. He turned the handle of the front door. It was locked. Jace frowned.

"Okay. I'll. . .I'll come back later."

Jace hesitated then stepped back from the red door with the welcome sign hanging slightly askew. He'd talked to her about carrying a side arm as well as finding extra security. In his mind the suggestion wasn't an option. Not anymore. He didn't want to be paranoid, but they lived in a world where people like Ricky weren't afraid to take advantage of an already devastating situation.

He looked down the street. What if Ricky had come here? What if he was here right now?

Two kids played in their yard a couple houses down while their father watched them. A dog barked. Birds chattered on power lines. Jace turned to the left. There was a white single-cab truck he hadn't seen before. It definitely hadn't been on this street the last time he'd come to see Morgan.

He started down the walk and stopped at the edge of the street. Mrs. Robinson had said she'd heard a vehicle outside her house the night of Jeremiah's murder. What if that hadn't been a figment of her imagination? It was possible. It wouldn't be the first time someone who'd managed to source fuel had driven through town. He kept his own truck drivable and had a stash of fuel locked up at the station for emergencies.

He headed around the back of the house, his gun drawn. There was no sign of Morgan's workers, but with over a dozen greenhouses, they could be anywhere on the large property. Clothes flapped on the line in the sunlight. The back veranda ran the length of the house and was covered for shade. Beneath it were chairs with colorful cushions, a mosaic-topped wrought iron table, and a toy box full of balls. But no sign of Morgan or Noah.

Jace glanced into one of the windows, trying to see what was going on inside, frowning at the curtains blocking his view. If he was wrong, and Morgan simply didn't want to see him, he'd deal with the consequences, but he wasn't leaving until he knew she was safe.

The back door opened. Ricky Addison stepped out, armed, with Noah in front of him. "Officer McQuaid, I presume."

Jace held his gun steady. "What's going on, Ricky?"

"You can put the weapon down. I'm just here to see my sister-in-law and nephew," Ricky said. "She told me how well you've been looking after her. I know it's been hard with my brother gone."

The gun to the back of Noah's head told a different story.

"Where's Morgan?" Jace said, catching the confusion in Noah's eyes.

"Bennett?" Ricky signaled to someone inside then turned back to Jace. "Morgan's fine. Like the boy said, he's just going hunting with me and a friend of mine. I thought Morgan could use a break, and Noah could use a change of scenery."

"I need to see Morgan," Jace repeated.

"She said she's busy right now. You heard her."

"Noah needs to stay here," Jace said, taking a step forward.

Out of the corner of his eye, Jace caught movement at the back door. A man—Bennett, Jace assumed—came barreling out of the house and headed straight toward Jace. He avoided the first punch, but felt the second slide across his jaw.

Jace landed the third punch straight to the man's thick gut, slowing him down, but only for a brief moment. Jace spun around to take off after Ricky and Noah. Bennett was faster. He grabbed Jace from behind, drove his elbow into his hip, then buckled his knee forward, forcing him down to the ground.

A horn blasted two times.

Bennett kicked Jace in the ribs, then took off around the side of the house.

Jace groaned, but forced himself to get up. He couldn't let Bennett get away. He grabbed a baseball from the wooden toy box and threw it as hard as he could at the man's feet, hitting him squarely in the ankles. Bennett tripped and fell forward.

Jace quickly grabbed the gun he'd dropped during the fight and pinned him down as the truck took off down the street. It was too late to stop Ricky from leaving, but if he could find out where he was going. . .

Jace flipped Bennett over onto his back, still holding the weapon on him. "He's leaving you behind. Where's he going?"

Bennett held his hands out in front of him in defeat. "I have no idea."

"Wrong answer."

Jace grabbed a zip tie out of his cargo pants, tied the man's hands together behind his back, then secured him with another tie to one of the legs of the wrought iron table.

Jace pulled out his radio to call his brother, but all he could get was static.

Morgan stumbled through the back door, her hands duct-taped together in front of her. "Jace, he's driving away. He's got Noah."

"I know," Jace said. "Are you okay?"

She nodded.

"We're going to get him back, I promise." He caught her gaze for a moment, then turned back to his radio. "Come on, Levi, come on. . ."

"Jace?"

He let out a sigh of relief at the sound of his brother's voice. "Ricky Addison just kidnapped Noah. I need you to sound the siren, then drive my truck to Morgan's house ASAP."

The line cracked.

"Levi?"

"Roger that," Levi said finally. "I'm on my way."

"Your truck still runs?" Morgan asked.

"Yes, but we need to know where Ricky's going," he said. He cut the tape off her wrists with his knife. "Does the family have a cabin around here?"

"I don't know, but Jace. . .Jace please. . ." She looked up at him as he freed her hands, tears in her eyes. "I can't lose Noah. He's all I have left."

"I know. And I promise, I'm going to do everything in my

power to get him back to you." He squeezed her hands. "Trust me."

Morgan nodded. "I do."

"I'm going to cut right to the chase," Jace said, bracing his hands against the table and staring Bennett straight in the eye. "We need to find Addison. I need to know where he's going. Obviously, he didn't care enough about you to wait, so giving him up will only help you."

"Or what?" Bennett leaned forward and laughed. "You have nothing on me. Why should I cooperate?"

"Because it's the right thing to do." Morgan's voice cracked as it rose. "Because my brother-in-law just took my child, and you're just as responsible for what happened in this house today."

"Listen." Bennett tugged on the zip tie. "I had no idea Ricky was going to grab the guns, or the boy for that matter, so you can't pin any of that on me."

"So you thought it was just a friendly visit to his brother's widow?" Jace asked.

"He told me it'd been a long time since he'd seen her, and he wanted to make sure she was okay. As for the guns, she offered to give him the guns. Everyone knows how dangerous it is out there."

"Cut the lies." Jace's voice rose. "We have evidence that you're a part of a gang, the Buffalo Riders. You've been tormenting towns, stealing food and supplies and then trading them on the black market. We've had a number of burglaries this past week including the warehouse and the bank explosion."

The man laughed. "How exactly are you going to do that? Run a face recognition program? You have no equipment or way to run suspects through a database. You can't even match my fingerprints, which means even if I were involved, you can't prove anything."

"Oh, you'd be surprised how much I can prove." Jace pulled Tess's sketches out of his back pocket, unfolded them, found the one he wanted, and set it on the table. "This looks an awful lot like you, including the scar above your eye."

A shadow crossed the man's face. "You're accusing me because of a sketch?" He tapped his finger against the picture. "This isn't proof."

"Oh, I've just gotten started. We found tobacco at the barn, the same licorice and fruit mixture I smell on you. Something that can easily be matched."

"Circumstantial." The man laughed, his cockiness back. "Like I said. You can't prove that I was involved in any of this."

Jace leaned forward. "Where's Ricky going?"

Bennett just shrugged.

Jace glanced at Morgan. The fear in her eyes emphasized the urgency of getting the information they needed. He needed to switch tactics.

"What did Ricky tell you was going to happen?" Jace asked, turning back to Bennett. "I'm guessing you're his muscle. Ricky probably told you there's really not anything I can do to hold you for long. He told you we don't have the resources to feed you and that all we can really do is try and run you out of town."

Bennett just stared at the mosaic tabletop.

"So you figure all you have to do is stop me from going after Ricky," Jace said, "knowing that in a couple hours you'll be sent out of town and free."

Bennett just shrugged.

Jace sat down in the chair across from Bennett. "He's wrong, you know."

"Who's wrong?"

"Ricky."

"What do you mean?"

Jace caught the worry in the man's eyes. "We might not have access to databases and fingerprint records, but that doesn't mean that the wheels of justice haven't adjusted to this new reality. Have you ever been to the salt mines?"

"No."

"It's backbreaking work and extremely dangerous." Jace leaned forward. "Did you know

that men convicted of crimes like murder are being used as slave labor in those mines?"

"Wait a minute." Bennett shook his head. "I had nothing to do with a murder."

"I have evidence that says otherwise."

"Oh no. The murder—that was all Ricky."

"So you *were* there when the barn was robbed."

"Ricky shot that man and then dumped the other guy into the springs. I never pulled the trigger."

"Nor did you try to stop him. Even before the Quake, you would have been charged and found guilty as an accessory."

The color drained from Bennett's face as he shifted in his chair.

"You have two choices," Jace said. "Take the murder rap and end up digging salt the rest of your life, or help me out and tell me where Ricky is."

Bennett stared out across the back acreage of the property. "He'll kill me."

"So which is worse? Running from Ricky, or spending the rest of your life working at hard labor?"

Bennett pressed his lips together, then let out a sharp breath. "There's a small casita

up on the mesa, about a half mile past Hangman's Ridge,

with a bunch of pecan trees out front. We've been staying there, but I can't guarantee that's where he went."

"One more thing," Jace said as he heard the roar of his truck. He grabbed a photo of Frank out of a pocket in his cargo pants. "Has this man been working with you?"

"Frank. . .yeah. I guess you could say that."

"Jace?"

"We're at the back of the house," Jace yelled, motioning for Morgan to come with him.

"Are you okay?" Levi asked as they rounded the corner.

"For now. We've got a prisoner tied up in the back. I need you to get him to the station then send out a search team on horseback to follow me up Hangman's Ridge. We'll stay in touch by radio, but that's where I think Ricky's gone. And Morgan, I promise you'll be the first to know as soon as we find Noah. And we will find him."

"Forget it," Morgan said. "I'm going with you."

"We can't even be sure where he is—"

"He took my son for leverage," Morgan said, starting for the truck. "Which means he wants something else. There's no way I'm going to sit here."

Jace ran after her, knowing there wasn't time to argue.

The enemy's surrounding me, God, and I don't know if I can keep her and Noah safe this time.

He drove in silence up the winding road that was flanked by evergreen trees and cabins scattered across the ridge. He wasn't used to the rumble of the vehicle, or the feel of the acceleration. With a limited fuel supply, this vehicle was for emergencies only. One, because the fuel was going to eventually run out, and two, road maintenance hadn't been on anyone's mind for almost a year, making travel extra dangerous. But if they were going to save Noah and catch up to Ricky, this was their only option.

Morgan clasped her hands in her lap. "Thank you. For showing up when you did."

"I thought you were ignoring me until you called me Officer McQuaid. I have to say that was clever." Jace frowned. "I'm just sorry I wasn't able to stop him."

"We will. You will. I should be better dealing with a crisis by now, but all of this. . ." She waved her hand in the air. "It's just so hard."

"You're doing a great job. I hope you know that. The greenhouses have helped sustain the town, and Noah. . . I'll just say you're raising a fine young man."

"I can't think about the future or what kind of life he's going to have. When I do, it terrifies me."

"You won't be alone."

The truck engine rumbled and he gave it more gas, praying they made it up the hill.

She dropped her gaze and pulled on a loose string from the hem of her yellow shirt. "I owe you an apology. All you've done to help me. I really do appreciate it. Even if you do worry about all the other single women in town."

Oh, I haven't fallen for any of the other single women. Only you.

Jace gripped the steering wheel. "No. I crossed the line. And for that I'm sorry."

"I didn't exactly dissuade you. It's just that. . ." She held out her ringless left hand.

"He took your ring?"

"Yes." She nodded. "And I'm terrified I'm about to lose everything else."

Grief was always complicated. He knew that firsthand. But whether or not she had feelings for him didn't change the fact that he was going to do whatever it took to keep his word and find her son.

CHAPTER TWENTY

MORGAN GRIPPED the armrest as Jace sped down the dirt road toward Hangman's Ridge. She took several slow deep breaths, trying to calm down, but couldn't shake the nausea. She glanced at the clock on the dash, surprised it had only been forty-five minutes since they'd left town. Every minute that passed knowing Noah was out there somewhere with Ricky felt like an eternity. And if Bennett was wrong or had lied to them, finding Noah was going to be harder than searching for a needle in a haystack.

The heavy numbness that had filled her for so long seemed to grow. She'd spent the last nine months moving on autopilot. Trying every day to make sure she and Noah had what they needed to survive as well as those around her. But this. . .this was her worst nightmare—something happening to Noah.

Her hand shook as she reached up and flipped the sun visor to block the light from her eyes. "Do you know how much farther?"

"It's been a long time since I've been up here, but I'd say less than a mile."

"Tommy and I used to hike on the other side of the ridge."

She stared out the window at the green foothills and thick brush. "The views of the mountains are spectacular."

"Did you ever stay overnight?"

"Not on purpose." A flood of memories surfaced. "But we did end up spending an unexpected night out because Tommy lost his way. Or at least that's how I always tell the story."

Jace laughed. "What happened?"

"We took a bad turn and ended up miles in the wrong direction," Morgan said, thankful for the distraction. "He always used to tease me that I carried too much in my pack. Which was true, but in my defense, I always had what we needed. That night we had my ultralight survival tent, a Firestarter, and freeze-dried pork fried rice."

"You would have been a good boy scout."

Her smile was automatic as they passed the sign for Hangman's Ridge, but did nothing to hide the anxiety that threatened to choke her. She leaned her head back and continued the prayer she'd been pouring out the last hour. The truck shook, and she heard a loud flapping noise coming from the rear. Jace turned the steering wheel to get the vehicle back on track, then came to a stop.

Morgan took off her seat belt. "Please, please don't tell me you have a flat tire."

Jace jumped out without answering. She met him at the back left tire, which was completely flat.

He kicked the hubcap, his jaw set with irritation. "I'm going to radio Levi and see how far they are behind us."

She glanced up the road, not willing to accept defeat. "We can't be far from the cabin."

Jace grabbed his backpack and radio from the cab. "I'm not getting a signal, but I might if we go higher. You up for a hike?"

"Definitely."

She started up the dirt road next to him, lost in her

thoughts. She knew he was worried about Noah, but she also knew Jace was worried about her. If she were honest, she missed someone worrying about her. Someone taking care of the little things around the house. Someone she could share her intimate thoughts and fears with.

A scream ripped through her thoughts. Jace grabbed his gun out of its holster and pushed her behind him. He walked forward a few steps, then stopped.

"You've got to be kidding me," he said, dropping his weapon to his side and turning back to Morgan.

"What is it?"

Morgan caught up to him and saw the group of Barbary sheep dart up the rocky hill. She pressed her hand against her heart. "I'd forgotten how loud those things can scream."

She scanned the ridge with a view of the town in the distance.

"Jace. . ." She jutted her chin to the left. "There's a casita ahead. That's got to be it."

A small house with corrugated metal siding sat in a clearing on the other side of the rocks, with a scattering of pecan trees and views of the valley below.

"I need to get closer to the house and see if I can verify who's inside, but we need to be careful," Jace said. "We might have to wait for Levi and the others before we go in."

They stayed in the shadows of the tree line as they made their way toward the house. A few voices broke the relative silence of the afternoon, and she could see movement through one of the windows. Jace stopped, then pointed ahead toward an elevated hunting blind partially covered by trees and overlooking several animal paths. He shook the ladder to make sure it was sturdy, then climbed up to check out the inside.

"I want you to wait up there for me," he said, stepping back off the ladder a moment later.

"Jace, I need to—"

"I'll be back." He reached out and squeezed her hand. "Trust me."

Morgan hesitated, wanting to go with him—desperate to find Noah—but at the same time, knowing he was right. She didn't have the experience he had to go up against Ricky and the others. Still, her anxiety intensified as she climbed up into the blind and watched from the open window. Jace slipped through the trees around the back of the house.

She pressed her lips together, drew in a deep breath, then blew it out. Like everyone she knew, the last year had left her feeling as if she were hanging from a thread—often unsure if she was going to survive another day. She knew her faith had helped to keep her from falling, but it was still so hard. She'd spent more time praying, had dug deeper into God's Word, and tried daily to keep her mind focused on Him. Determined to trust Him no matter what happened. But this. . .this was so hard.

A rustling below pulled her from her thoughts. Jace climbed up the ladder and sat down next to her.

"What did you see?" she asked.

"I was able to look through one of the side windows. I saw Noah, and he looked fine. He was playing with some toy cars."

She caught his gaze, feeling the urgency to do something. "We need to get Noah out of there."

"We will, but we need to wait for Levi and the sheriff and the others. I didn't see Frank, but I did see Ricky, and there are at least five others. I don't want to take a chance of risking Noah's life."

Morgan sat back against the wall and squeezed her eyes shut for a moment, trying to stop the tears. "I'm sorry, I'm just so scared. I saw Ricky's eyes when he left. All he cares about is his survival. He doesn't care about what happens to my son."

She let him pull her against his chest and wrap his arms around her. She could feel his warm breath against her face. Felt her body relax as she leaned into him. Her faith might have helped keep her from falling, but she missed the physical presence of someone in her life. The physical touch of someone who loved her.

"Can I ask you something?" She wiped the tears from her face, sat back, and looked up at him. "Why is it so important for you to protect me—to protect this town, even though you never planned to stay?"

Her question must have caught him off guard. She could see the surprise in his expression.

"I don't know, I guess. . .I guess it's because even though I can't change the past, I can at least try to change the present." He shifted next to her, but kept his arm around her. "I fought so hard against stepping up and taking this job. Tried to bargain with my father. Tried to bargain with God. Told Him there were other people who could do far better than I ever could. But in the end I didn't really feel like I had a choice."

"None of us have had a say to any of this," she said, her voice barely above a whisper.

"I'm sorry, Morgan. You lost so much—"

"I'm not minimizing what you've gone through." She looked up at him, trying to clarify. "And I don't want you to feel sorry for me. I only say that because I understand. I understand what it's like to have life turn in a direction that you never wanted or asked for."

"If you'd told me a year ago that I would be leading up the town's law enforcement, I would've laughed. I'd planned to leave the service and never do any type of law enforcement again. Ever."

She reached out and squeezed his hand. "What happened, Jace?"

He stared out the window toward the house for a moment before finally answering. “There were always certain things about my job. . .certain things that I’ve never been able to get out of my mind. That one situation you can’t erase, no matter how hard you try not to hang on to the memories. It’s always there, hovering just beneath the surface.”

She understood exactly what he meant. “The moment they told me Tommy was dead replays in my mind over and over.”

“I haven't told anyone here what happened that day. Not even my father.” Jace drew in a deep breath and blew it out slowly. "We brought in a prisoner, and my job was to gather as much information as I could from him. Information was key to keeping the area safe and stopping future attacks. He was young, late twenties, and scared. I thought I could read him. I asked questions, listened, and did all the things I was trained to do. I thought I had broken him and gotten what I needed out of him.”

“But you didn't?”

Jace shook his head. “Turns out he lied about everything. The weaponry, the location, everything. Because of that mistake, we were unable to stop the next attack. We lost three of our men and four civilians in a bomb blast.”

“Oh, Jace, I can’t even imagine what you felt—and still do—but that wasn't your fault.”

“It was completely my fault. I misread him.” Jace pulled away from her and moved closer to the window to get a better view of the house. “If I hadn’t been so cocky about it, if I’d taken the time to ensure I had the right information, those people would be alive today.”

“You’re anything but cocky, Jace McQuaid. I'm sorry for what happened, but nobody gets it right every time.”

“You didn't have to contact their wives and children. Watch

their faces as the horrible truth that they would never see their loved ones again seeped in."

"I'm sorry. I truly am. I know that doesn't really help, but I think you need to forgive yourself. You can't change the situation, but you can change the present."

"I'm not sure I can do that."

Morgan wrapped her arms around her chest. "I guess we all have our regrets. Tommy was late for work that morning. We got in an argument. I was upset about something stupid. Told him I was tired of always picking up after him. Told him the least he could do was clean up the garage when he was done out there. Now I'd do anything to see that mess."

"You're right." He sat back down next to her, seemingly lost in thought. "Maybe it's time for both of us to try and put aside our regrets and create something new with what we have right in front of us."

Like whatever's happening between you and me?

She licked her dry lips, trying to ignore the implications of the question along with his statement, but couldn't. Because maybe, just maybe, he was right.

"Morgan. . ." Jace motioned her toward the window of the hunting blind. "It looks like they've decided to pack up."

She moved to where she could get a closer view, then pressed her hand against her heart. "How long until your brother and the others get here?"

"I'd say at least twenty minutes. . .maybe more."

"We have to get Noah out before they move again. If Ricky takes him from here, I'll never see him again."

"I'm not going to let that happen," Jace said. "I have a plan."

Her eyes narrowed as she tried to read his expression. "What kind of plan?"

"How would you like to fly off this mountain?"

"With your paraglider?"

Jace nodded. "I happen to have it in the back of my truck."

She held up her hand. "You're not paragliding off this mountain with me and my son. That's the most ridiculous thing I've ever heard."

"Why is it so crazy? We don't have a lot of choices. We can't drive down, it's too far to walk, and once they start looking for us, they're going to move a lot faster."

"Jace." She closed her eyes for a moment and drew in a deep breath. "Have you always been this way?"

"What way is that?"

"Having the ability to come up with some harebrained idea and getting everyone to go along with it."

"So you agree?" he asked.

"How dangerous is it? Flying with three people?"

"I've logged hundreds of hours and know what I'm doing, Morgan. I wouldn't have even suggested it if I didn't think it was safe. You have to believe that."

Her hands tremored as she caught his gaze. "I believe you're a magnet for

trouble."

At least you are with my heart.

She swallowed hard. "What do you want me to do?"

"We're going to have to move fast." Jace handed her the keys to his truck and then unzipped his backpack and pulled out a package of fireworks.

"Wait a minute," she said. "You just happen to carry not only equipment to paraglide, but also a roll of firecrackers in your bag?"

Jace chuckled. "Let's just say I've had to learn to be resourceful and prepared for anything. And right now, we need a distraction."

"So what do you need me to do?"

"You're going to set these off right behind the tree line to our right," Jace said. "That will give us about a minute of what they'll think is gunfire."

She nodded, trying not to think about all the things that could go wrong. Or what would happen if they couldn't get Noah.

Please, God. . .we need you right now.

"As soon as they start going off, I want you to go back to the truck. Don't stick around. In the bed of the truck, under the canopy, there's a large bag. I want you to pull it out and lay it on the ground, then wait for me."

She glanced back at the house where the men had started moving bags and boxes and stacking them up on a large cart. "And in the chaos of the firecrackers, you're going to go in and grab Noah?"

"There's a back door, and I'm hoping I can slip in and out and grab him without being noticed."

She blew out a sharp breath, praying again that his plan would work, then climbed out of the blind with the firecrackers and a lighter.

Morgan quickly laid out the firecrackers like he'd told her, careful to stay behind the trees where Ricky and his men couldn't see her from where they were working at the front of the house. She spun the spark wheel on the lighter, but the flame just flickered in the wind, and the fuse didn't catch. Hands shaking, she tried a second time. Nothing. A third strike of the lighter and the fuse finally caught. She took a step back as the first cracker went off, followed by a string of loud pops. Her heart pounded as she turned and ran toward the truck. She couldn't look back. Couldn't think about the worst-case scenario if Jace got caught or if he couldn't get to Noah.

The bag was in the bed of the truck just like he'd told her. She knew nothing about paragliding beyond what he'd told Noah back at the house. She also hadn't wanted to tell him how heights terrified her and that diving was as close to flying as she'd ever planned to get outside of an airplane. But if the last year had taught her anything, it had taught her to be bold and that she could do far more than she'd ever thought she could.

She unzipped the bag and laid it out on the ground as best she could, then stepped back from the equipment. He'd told her to trust him, but trusting him with her son's life was almost as terrifying as trusting him with her heart.

She looked in the direction of the house, searching for movement and the flash of red from Noah's shirt. She'd taught him from a young age when it was appropriate to talk to strangers and when it wasn't. But in trying to protect Noah from the truth about his uncle, she'd ended up endangering him.

She glanced at her watch, then started pacing and praying at the same time. Praying for miraculous intervention as Jace tried to rescue her son. Praying that God would put an end to this nightmare. Another minute passed. She kept pacing, then turned around. Jace and Noah were running toward her.

"Did they see you?" she asked, running to them.

"I don't think so," Jace said, "but it isn't going to take long for them to notice he's missing. We need to get off this bluff."

Morgan kneeled down in front of Noah and wrapped her arms around him. "Are you okay?"

Noah nodded, then frowned. "I didn't know Uncle Ricky was a bad man. I told him I wanted to go home, but he said I couldn't. He said I was a. . .a lever."

"Leverage." Morgan choked out the word. "But you're really okay?"

Noah shrugged. "It was just boring. I played while they talked about adult stuff." His attention shifted to Jace, clearly unaware of just how dangerous the situation really was. "Can I watch?"

"Of course you can," Jace said.

Noah clapped, his eyes wide with excitement. "We're going to fly!"

"It's actually a lot like flying an airplane," Jace said, working quickly to lay out the canopy and adjust the lines. "Just like the pilot has a safety list before he takes off, I have one too. I have to check the wing for any damage and making sure my lines aren't tangled. And I have to make sure it's a safe place to take off, and that the wind is right." He pulled out a helmet and handed it to Morgan. "We're going to take off from the other side of the road where there is a good slope before the terrain drops down."

Jace quickly worked to get the equipment together and ready them for take-off. "I'll be behind you and will secure Noah in front of you. You'll both be strapped in, so you can't fall, but I'm going to need you to run with me, Morgan."

She nodded. "Okay."

He looked at her and mouthed "Trust me" before getting into position behind her. Morgan nodded, then closed her eyes.

"Start running," Jace shouted.

Morgan obeyed, her eyes still shut. Seconds later, the wind caught the canopy and pulled them up. Noah squealed with delight in front of her.

"Mom, can you see the eagle?"

Morgan opened her eyes for the first time as they soared off the ridge and over the valley. "It is beautiful."

"Have you ever seen anything like this, Morgan?" Jace's breath tickled her ear as he spoke.

"No. Never. It's like flying underwater, except you can see so much farther."

"One day I'll bring you up here when you're not running from the Buffalo Riders."

Below them was a stunning combination of vast open grasslands, wooded canyons, and forested hills, all with the rugged mountains as a backdrop. Jace shifted directions, and her stomach flipped, but the views were stunning.

They landed about a mile outside Shadow Ridge on open grassland surrounded by gray oaks, alligator junipers, and piñon pine, and a wooded creek to the south.

She let out a whoosh of air as she struggled to find her balance. "Are you okay, Noah?"

"You bet. That was so awesome. I can't wait to tell my friends."

Jace grabbed her arm and helped her out of the harness. "What about you? Are you okay?"

"A little shaky, but I'm fine."

"And safe now, Morgan."

"I know, but Jace—"

His radio went off, and she motioned for him to go ahead and answer it. They might have gotten Noah back, but Ricky was still out there.

"It's Levi," Jace said, then walked ahead of them a few steps.

She helped Noah retie his shoes, then pulled him against her, grateful he was safe.

"Mom?"

"Yeah, babe," she said.

"If I could have a new daddy, I wouldn't mind having Jace."

"A new daddy?"

She glanced back at Jace, the man who had stepped into her life and shaken it upside down. Who refused to stop until he knew she was safe. And who'd even managed to capture her son's heart.

And hers?

She'd never imagined falling for someone else. That had never been a part of her plan. But then neither had diving for a dead body, being robbed by her brother-in-law, or someone kidnapping her son.

"I just radioed someone in town and they are on their way with a couple of horses," Jace said, starting to pack up the glider.

She worked with him to fold up the glider, following his directions and amazed at how he managed to put it all back in the pack.

"Think you might want to go flying with me again one day?" Jace asked, standing up and brushing off his pants.

"I will!" Noah shouted as he ran past them, then stopped. "Someone's coming."

Jace put his hand on Noah's head. "It's Hernandez."

"Is he a good guy?"

"Yes." Jace glanced at Morgan. "He definitely is."

Jace had just finish packing up the paraglider equipment when Hernandez came into view riding his horse and leading two other mares.

"Hernandez, I can't tell you how glad I am to see you," Jace said as he reached out and shook the man's hand.

"Are you guys okay?" Hernandez asked in return.

Jace held up his hand to block the sun from his eyes. "We're fine, but what about the team that was sent up there? Any news?"

"I just received a radio message from the sheriff—"

"Hang on." Jace pulled his binoculars out of his pocket, then turned to Noah. "Are you up for a very important job?"

Noah's eyes widened as he nodded.

"I need a scout."

"What are we looking for?" Noah asked, lowering his voice to a whisper. "Bears?"

"I don't think we have to worry about bears, but you do

know that Thanksgiving and Christmas are coming soon, right?"

That question produced a smile. "Yes."

Jace handed him the binoculars. "I need a turkey for Thanksgiving, and this spot right here, well, I've been told that sometimes, if you look really hard, you can find them here."

"Yes sir!" Noah held up the binoculars and started his search.

Morgan mouthed "Thank you" as the three of them moved away a few steps so Noah didn't overhear their conversation.

"They got to the cabin about ten minutes ago," Hernandez said. "Ricky and his gang were in the process of packing up the last wagon."

"Did they get him?" Morgan asked.

Hernandez shook his head. "I'm sorry, but no. He and two others got away."

Jace turned to Morgan. "Then you and Noah aren't safe."

"You don't think he'd come back here, do you?" Morgan's hands fisted at her sides. "It seems to me he'd try to get as far away as possible."

"Maybe, but I don't want to take any chances," Jace said, "What about Frank? Did you find him?"

"You won't believe this," Hernandez said, "but Frank showed up about fifteen minutes after you all had left and turned himself in at the station."

Jace took a step back. "What?"

"He claims he escaped and it was all a setup. He said other men killed Jeremiah and Keaton. Says they used him as a scapegoat."

"That doesn't make sense," Jace said. "He held a gun to Keaton's head."

"Frank claims the gun wasn't loaded and that they threatened to hurt his family if he didn't play along. Keaton was their inside man. They needed a distraction for the explosion and someone to frame. If he's telling the truth, it worked."

Morgan saw the confusion playing out in Jace's expression and knew it was going to take a while to untangle the truth of the questionable scenario.

Jace turned to Morgan. "I don't know if I believe him, but until we find the rest of them, I want you and Noah to stay out at the ranch. It will be safer there."

She started to argue, then stopped, knowing he was right. And knowing she wasn't willing to take any chances with her son's life.

"Morgan, I can take you and Noah to the ranch and get you set up there," Hernandez said. "Jace, the sheriff isn't sure how long their radio batteries are going to last, but he'll do his best to keep you updated. He also wants you to interview Frank."

"Did he leave any law presence in town?"

"Me along with a couple of others."

Morgan waited until Jace finished talking to Hernandez, then wrapped her arms around his neck in a big hug.

"I know things are about to get really busy for you," she whispered in his ear. "But thank you."

He looked down at her, clearly surprised by her action, but that didn't stop a smile from spreading across his face. "You're welcome."

"Oh, and Jace. . ." She took a step back then caught his gaze again. "What did you plan to do if Noah actually spotted a turkey?"

Jace shot her a wry grin and shrugged. "Honestly, I hadn't thought that far ahead."

Her heart raced as he gave her that familiar look that melted her heart. She had a feeling that things were never going to be the same again.

DAY 277

CHAPTER TWENTY-ONE

THE SUN WAS ABOUT to set when Jace stepped out of the station and locked the door behind him. If he hurried, he might actually make it to the community talent show that had been planned for tonight. The last ten days had kept him busy as he substantiated Frank's innocence, worked with the sheriff and his men to capture the last of the Buffalo Riders, and planned tomorrow's demolition of the bank. But his thoughts had never been too far from Morgan.

He'd missed her.

"Officer McQuaid?"

Jace slipped the keys into his pocket and turned around. "Gideon. It's good to see you."

"Are you headed to the town talent show at the Williams' place?"

"I am." Jace hesitated. "Unless you need something?"

"No. I have something for you, actually, a *tres leches* cake from my mother." He held up

a package. "She said it's not much, but she does appreciate all you did to help find out the truth about my father and bring him home."

"She knows how much I love her cake, but please tell her that she doesn't owe me anything. Knowing that your father is both innocent and okay is enough. Really."

"I know. But I think it makes her feel better."

"Then tell her thank you for me."

"I will."

Jace took the gift and started to leave, then stopped. "Gideon, your father told me you've been putting in extra volunteer hours at the warehouse."

"Yeah. I mean, he sees this town as something important to help save, and I guess. . .I guess I've decided he's right." Gideon shoved his hands into his pockets. "And you were right too."

"How's that?"

"You reminded me that I can't spend my life waiting for this to be over. I have to find out how to live in the middle of it. Maybe it is just a season, but if I sit around and do nothing, then that's what I'll get in return."

"Those are pretty profound words. I'm proud of you." Jace rested his hands on his belt. "You know, Gideon, a few months ago, I went to the warehouse to check on security. I spoke with your father for a few minutes, and he started bragging about you."

"Really?" Gideon's eyes lit up. "About what?"

"He'd taken you out shooting and was impressed with your skills. Life has changed, but there's always a need for strong people of integrity."

"I'm doing my best. I really am."

"Here's the deal. I'm needing to add to the department. It doesn't pay much, unless you count chickens, eggs, and, if you're lucky, an occasional *tres leches* cake." Jace chuckled. "You'd start at the bottom, but it would be good experience."

"You're serious?"

"I am."

Gideon shook his head as if he was trying to process what he'd just been told. "I would

love that, but why me?"

"I see myself in you. Everyone deserves a second chance. You'd have to clear it with your parents, and there would be a trial period with rules that would have to be followed—"

"I can do that. Anything you say. I'm in."

"Okay." Jace held out his hand. "With your parents' permission, consider it an official invite."

Twenty minutes later, Jace slipped inside the barn and found an empty seat toward the back as Morgan walked up onto the stage at the front with her guitar. This had been her idea, a gathering of homegrown talent and entertainment that the town had responded to enthusiastically. The large barn on the outskirts of town had once been used as a wedding venue. Tonight it had been set up with dozens of tables covered with white tablecloths, and a stage had been built up front with pallets. Candles and lanterns lit up the room, and long tables held the refreshments that would be served at the end of the talent show.

The audience was filled with familiar faces. The sheriff and his men, including the one who had been shot by the Buffalo Riders, were sitting near the front on the left. Jace's father, Tess, and Hope sat a bit farther back with Margaret. His attention shifted back to the stage. He was later than he'd wanted to be, but at least he hadn't missed her song.

Morgan sat down on a stool, then started strumming her guitar in a halo of yellow light. "Before I sing, I want to thank each of you for coming out tonight. I can truly say that it's been a successful evening so far, filled with a lot of laughs and a lot of wonderful talent." She scanned the audience until their eyes met. She held Jace's gaze for a moment before looking away, her cheeks pink in the glow of the candlelight. "Until this last week it had been a long time since I played my guitar, but someone recently reminded me that sometimes we have to put aside our regrets and create something new with what we have right in front of us. That's what I want tonight to be. My father loved listening to Louis Armstrong and especially the song, *What a Wonderful World*. And although the choice might seem odd to some of you, I think if you listen to the words, you'll discover it really is the perfect reminder for us tonight."

Her mellow voice drew him in as she sang the classic hit with its simple lyrics and soulful tune. He'd been wrong to ever doubt his feelings. He loved her and needed to tell her. Because even in a world that had fallen apart at the seams, everything somehow still seemed wonderful when he was around her.

The audience erupted into applause as she left the stage and headed to the back of the room, past shadows from the candlelight flickering against the barn wall.

"Next up we have a somewhat unconventional duet who will be performing a magic trick as their talent for this evening. . ."

The emcee introduced the next act, but all Jace saw was Morgan. She put her guitar away in its case, then walked over to his table and sat down in the empty seat next to him.

"That was beautiful," he said, taking in her jeans, boots, white shirt, and colorful shawl.

You're beautiful.

"I haven't seen you for a while," she said, leaning closer to him while the audience had their attention on the stage. "I just wanted to make sure you were okay."

Jace glanced at the door. "Do you want to go for a walk?"

He held his breath, not knowing what her reaction would be. Not knowing how his heart would handle the rejection if she made it clear that their kiss had been a mistake.

"Yeah. I would." Her smile tripped his heart. "They don't really need me here anymore."

He fought the urge to take her hand as they stepped out of the barn and down the dirt path beneath a sea of stars toward the open field behind them.

"You should be flattered, you know," she said, pulling her shawl closer around herself.

"Why's that?"

"I just chose you over Margaret's pecan pie."

Jace laughed. "You still might be able to snag yourself a piece, but I won't take your yes for granted. The last two weeks have been hectic, to say the least. Which is also why I wanted to apologize."

"For what?" Morgan asked.

"I should have come talk to you days ago, and I would have, except every time I tried to get away, there was someone or something demanding my time."

"I just hope that with the Buffalo Riders behind bars now, hopefully you'll be able to catch your breath."

And spend more time with you.

He wondered if she was thinking what he was, that once again this was the calm before the storm. But right now, whatever was coming next didn't matter. All that mattered was the fact that she was here with him.

"You really are talented, Morgan."

"Thank you. It's been so long since I've done anything. . .anything normal. It felt good. Though I didn't think you were going to be able to come."

"I wasn't sure I was going to either. The sheriff's leaving at first light with his men and the prisoners. I had to make sure everything was ready for their trip."

"You've got to be exhausted."

"It has been a long couple of weeks, but we caught them all. Even Ricky."

"And I'm grateful. It's allowed me to breathe a bit easier."

She stopped and looked up to him. "We could sit down. The sky is amazing tonight."

"You won't be too cold?"

She pulled off her large shawl. "I don't think I'll have to worry about that tonight."

He watched as she spread her shawl on the grass, trying not to interpret from her words something that wasn't there.

"Did Noah come tonight?" he asked, sitting down next to her. Their arms barely touched in the moonlight.

"He's at a sleepover with a friend. We've had a few ups and downs, but he's doing better. Especially considering he wanted to go. Since Ricky took him, he hasn't wanted to leave my side. Says he has to protect me. Sound familiar?" She smiled up at him. "I know we've got a long road ahead of us—we all do—but I think he's going to be okay."

"He's a great kid, but he also has a great mom. What you did for the town tonight is huge."

"I had a lot of help. Margaret, Tess, Hope, Sofia, and Judith. . . They all pitched in. I think it's going to be something we do every month. The town needs something to look forward to."

He stared up at the night sky. It had always been stunning, but now, completely void of any lights from the town, it was even more spectacular. A view of the Milky Way loomed above them, so close he felt as if he could reach out and touch it. A blanket of diamonds for the taking.

He pulled his compact binoculars out of his pocket and searched the sky for Jupiter and its moons.

She nudged him. "I guess I'm not the only one prepared for anything."

"Take a look," he said, handing them to her. "It's amazing how everything down here has changed and yet the sun still rises and the moon still shines at night."

"Because His faithfulness stands fast. Never changing."

She stared up at the stars a moment longer, then turned to him. "Thank you. For reminding me once again that there's still beauty around us. That we just have to stop and look for it."

"And I have to admit, it's really nice to share it with someone."

The moonlight caught her expression as she turned to him. "I'm working on it, but it still scares me, not knowing what tomorrow holds."

"I agree, but I'm realizing that we've never known what tomorrow holds."

She let out a low chuckle and handed him the binoculars. "True, though I like to think I'm in control."

"It's funny how we always thought it was a guarantee that our alarms would go off every morning, we'd get out of bed, turn on the coffeemaker, take a hot shower, and drive to work. Now we see everything from a different perspective because we know that isn't true. All of a sudden, we can't call anyone or check the internet. We don't even know if we'll have enough food to get through the winter." He slipped the binoculars back inside his pocket. "But like you said, it's not all negative. I'm sitting beneath the stars with the most beautiful woman in Shadow Ridge."

"Jace."

"I do believe you're blushing."

Her gaze dropped. "It's been a long time since a man has given me a compliment."

"I know you miss Tommy. I know that losing him is probably the hardest thing you've ever gone through, and I'm not asking you to stop feeling or hurting—"

"Jace—"

"Please. Just let me finish," he said, afraid he'd lose his courage. "I hope I'm not totally out of line, but Morgan, I'm falling in love with you, and all I can do is hope you feel something for me."

He could hear live fiddle music coming from the barn and bits of light shining through the cracks in the walls—but all he could see was Morgan.

"I still miss Tommy," she said finally. "For so long I didn't think I could function without him. I didn't know how. I was suddenly a single mom in a world I didn't understand. I'm not the same person I used to be. None of us are. But now. . ."

He sat still, not wanting her to feel pressured or rushed.

"Noah always asks me when you're coming over," she said. "I've always told him that you help all the widows in town."

"I do, but I'm only in love with one of them."

She braced her hands behind her and stared at the sky. "I've thought about the possibility of us. Every time you bring me something, I always hope it's not just because you feel sorry for me. And sometimes. . .sometimes when you walk into a room, my heart pounds and I realize that I'm starting to feel again. Something that both excites and terrifies me. "

"What are you saying, Morgan?"

She leaned into him. "I'm saying I really want you to kiss me."

He cupped his hand behind her head and pulled her toward him. He felt a fire stirring inside him as he brushed his lips across hers, then deepened the kiss. This relationship was unexpected. Even at times unwanted. But he'd fought his feelings for too long, and all the excuses he'd piled up had slipped away. Life might have changed, but whatever happened, he knew he wanted to spend it with her.

Morgan pulled away a moment later out of breath, and sat back, still looking at him in the moonlight.

"What happens next?" she whispered.

"What do you want to happen next?"

"I was thinking that we probably should start with an official date."

"Agreed but that has to be more than my stopping by with seeds for you or licorice for Noah. I do that for all the single women, remember."

She laughed. "Do you ask all of them on a date?"

"Oh no," he said, taking her hand. "Because there's only one woman I intend on taking out on a date."

She laced her fingers with his. "Good."

There was one other question he had to ask her. "Do you think Noah is going to mind?"

"Oh, I happen to know that he approves of the idea."

"Good," he echoed, pulling her hand against his chest. "Because someone reminded me recently of the importance of living life to the fullest no matter what's happening around us. And if you ask me, right now it's a pretty wonderful world."

EPILOGUE

TWO HOURS LATER, Jace dropped Morgan off at her door and headed back down Main Street, still feeling the good-night kiss she'd left him with. While he still might now know what the future held, any doubts he'd had about their relationship had vanished. A coyote howled in the distance, reminding him that dangers still lurked around them. They'd caught Ricky and the rest of his men, but the reality was that this was far from over.

The significance of his duties still hung over him, but he was determined not to move forward alone. The officers he'd put into place were already making a difference, and he'd spoken to pastor Matthew again about working together to help those in town who'd fallen through the cracks.

A flash of light caught his attention as he passed the bank. The remaining structure was finally going to be taken down tomorrow, so the only person who should be here was Hernandez who was guarding the structure tonight.

"Hernandez?"

The light went off.

Strange.

Jace pulled his gun out from its holster and turned his own

flashlight on the pile of rubble. The light caught movement near the sidewalk.

"Hernandez?"

The man groaned and rolled over.

Jace crouched down beside him and helped him sit up. "What happened?"

Hernandez rubbed the back of his head. "I don't know. They came from behind and knocked me out. Didn't even see it coming. I'm sorry."

"It's okay. I want you to stay right here. I'll be back."

Jace leveled his gun out in front of him and ducked underneath the crime scene tape they'd set up. He'd known it was dangerous, keeping the structure up this long, but they'd needed time to return as much as they could from the safety deposit boxes and vault to the owners as well as formulate a plan to safely demolish the building.

He walked carefully across what used to be the lobby, his boots crunching on the ground. Movement caught his eye again.

Jace pointed his gun and light at the figure, then stopped. "Lois. . .what are you doing here?"

She took a step back from the safe, then held up her hands. "Does it matter?"

"What do you mean? I thought all of this was cleaned out."

She waved her hands higher. "Not all of it. Owen lied. I lied. I thought I could find it before you tear this all down tomorrow."

Jace's light caught the bottle of moonshine in the shadows. "Lois, are you drunk?"

"He lied to me." Her voice rose as she stumbled forward, confirming his theory. "He used me. And I thought Ricky loved me."

"Why do you need into the vault?"

"It's my only way out of here."

"What's in there?"

She shrugged. "Drugs buried in this rubble. Ricky never got everything he came for. "

Jace worked to put the pieces together. "You were trafficking drugs for him?"

"Drugs. . .money. He told me it was the perfect set up really. No one would ever guess that a bank teller was involved. It wasn't hard."

"Didn't Owen know?"

Lois pressed her finger against her lips and smiled. "I had to keep his secret about his affair. I'm good at getting things out of people. I listen. You can't blame me for using the information I gain."

"So you turned a bank vault into your own private safe."

"The Quake ruined everything for me. I was planning to move away from here. I'd saved enough money to get out of this hole. No one appreciated me. I was just the friendly teller who took everyone's money. What they didn't know is that I was listening. I overheard conversations. Knew things. I know a lot of things."

"What kind of things?"

Lois let out a low laugh but held out her hands. "You're so naive. Ricky might have deceived me, but all of this is only the tip of the iceberg."

"What do you mean?"

"Stopping Ricky. . .stopping me. . .neither is going to change anything because you have a much bigger problem. What do you think happens when the world shuts down? Do you really think that the demand for drugs, young girls, and sex diminishes? Think of all the girls who are no longer in school and who have nowhere safe to go." She stepped forward, close enough that he could smell the alcohol on her breath. "And it's too late to stop the darkness."

YOU'VE JUST FINISHED the stunning conclusion of Survival, book one on the Fallout Series. Don't miss the rest of this heart-pounding series!

HUNTED SNEAK PEEK

HUNTED: CHAPTER ONE

OCTOBER 10TH, DAY 296

"PULL the string back a little further. Aim. Then release the arrow as if your life depended on it."

Ava Solomon squared her hips, gripping the bow with her left hand like Levi McQuaid had told her, then pulled slowly back on the string, keeping her eyes on the orange pumpkin target. A warm breeze swept across her face as she breathed in the scent of smoke from the cooking fires tingeing the desert winds.

She'd always loved this region framed by mountains in the distance. Shadow Ridge was just one of a dozen small, isolated towns spread out across west Texas where wide open desert prairies filled with scrub brush and cactus met winding mountain roads and led to higher elevations. Rugged, untamed landscapes, filled with backcountry wildlife, where the stars hung like lanterns at night, almost close enough to touch.

For the past decade, though, Shadow Ridge had simply become a place for her to visit. It held memories, but it had never been where she intended to settle down for the rest of her life.

Until the Quake.

The instant the grid went down, everything in her world changed. No power grid meant no electricity, no internet, no streaming movies, no way to schedule an Uber or send a text message. It meant she couldn't hop on an airplane and fly back to her life in Houston where she worked as a cryptanalyst by day and an aspiring author by night. While she might have inherited her love of language from her Nigerian father and her love of books from her Irish mother, she'd never embraced their love of hunting and outdoor adventure. That was her sister Josie.

Instead, she'd grown up in a world where books were her escape. When her father had managed to convince her to go hiking with him, he'd tell her stories of growing up in the African bush and share his wealth of knowledge of west Texas flora and fauna—the place that had become his home after thirty years of managing one of the local ranches. Her mother had taught her how to make Irish stew and soda bread, and encouraged her in her writing endeavors.

Now she wished she'd listened more.

Because suddenly it was her responsibility to raise her seventeen-year-old sister and keep food on the table for the two of them. In an effort to help them make it through the winter, she'd learned everything she could about raising chickens and rabbits, water glassing fresh eggs, and growing a garden beneath the hot, west Texas sun. They washed clothes in the round pink swimming pool and had perfected her father's rainwater catchment system for harvesting water.

Ava blew out a sharp breath, her mind spinning as she shifted her thoughts back to what Levi had taught her. Stance. .

.posture. . .position. . .The tension inside her built as she stared at the target, the muscles in her arm and shoulder tight.

"Bring your hand slowly to your neck. . ." Levi stepped up next to her, lowering her elbow slightly. "Relax, you're doing fine, Ava."

She blew out another sharp breath as Levi's earlier words replayed in her mind.

Release the arrow as if your life depended on it.

She swallowed hard. She wasn't doing fine because he was right. Her life and the life of her sister depended on her. She might baby her garden and try to make friends with the hens who gave them eggs, but while speaking four languages sounded impressive to some, it hadn't prepared her for living off the grid.

She pulled the arrow back another half inch, then released it. The arrow launched at an angle, missing the target by a yard.

She dropped the bow to her side, trying to hold back the tears. "I can't do this, Levi."

"Yes, you can." He handed her another arrow. "You just need to relax."

Funny. She hadn't relaxed for months.

She'd lost count of how many days had passed since the grid had gone down—"the Quake" as everyone in Shadow Ridge had come to call it. She used to keep her schedule meticulously organized in her head. But now the days and weeks had merged together into a time warp, blurring her memories until she couldn't remember what she'd had for breakfast most days.

It wasn't just the fact that she couldn't hunt or that her garden wasn't thriving as she'd hoped. Raising a teenager was proving difficult. Josie had always been stubborn, but the past year had changed her. She'd become more and more argumentative, and while she did what Ava asked her to do—most of the time—she'd made it clear that she had no desire to take orders from her older sister.

"Ava. . ." Levi touched her arm. "I think you're trying too hard."

She squeezed back the tears, her lips quivering. "Trying too hard and failing isn't going to put dinner on my table. Maybe I just need to stick to chickens and rabbits. I can't do this."

Levi set the bow on the picnic table, then took her hand and led her over to the wooden swing her father had built at the back of the house. "What's really going on? Something tells me this isn't just about your inability to shoot a pumpkin."

The ridiculous-sounding sentence brought an unsolicited smile to her lips.

"Have you not noticed how bad I am?" She nodded toward the arrows scattered across the back yard, none of which had made it even close to the target.

He squeezed her fingers. "That wasn't an answer to my question."

Simmering anger rose to the surface. "If I can't shoot a pumpkin, how am I supposed to shoot an animal that's running? It's this whole mess." She waved her arms. "This can't continue forever. I need something normal. Anything. A scoop of Blue Bell ice cream. . .a hot soak in the tub. . .pumpkin spice coffee." She sighed. "Boy, I could really use some pumpkin spice coffee right now."

He sat quietly beside her, letting her pour out the pent up frustration. Patient, with no judgment in his eyes. Just like he'd always done.

"I just can't do this anymore." She lowered her voice in defeat. "My mother is dead, and I have no idea how to help my sister. You've spent your whole life learning how to shoot, learning how to track, learning how to hunt. I've spent my life with my nose in a book. I don't know how to do this. That's why things have to go back to normal. I refuse to think otherwise. Because *this*. . .this isn't the life I want."

The childish string of words came out before she could filter them.

"I get it more than you think," he said, squeezing her hand.

"I know." She looked up at him, wishing she could take the words back. "I'm sorry. I know none of us want this life."

"You have nothing to be sorry about, but think about it this way. What if you hadn't been here when all this happened? Your sister needs you, and you were able to be with your mother before she died. I think you're exactly where you need to be."

Ava pressed her lips together, her shoulders slumped as fatigue mingled with the feelings of heavy loss. "I don't know."

"You wouldn't have gotten that extra time to spend with your mother. Your sister would be here by herself. Your being here matters. You've made a difference to your family, to this town, to me. . ."

"You always know what to say." She shook her head and leaned back against the swing, his hand still clasping hers. It was true. Levi McQuaid had always been there for her. Listening and never judging. "I know I'm overreacting, but Josie has started sneaking out of the house at night, which isn't like her. I'm pretty sure she's gotten involved with the wrong kids, and I don't know how to stop it."

"So your frustration really is more than a failure to hit a pumpkin with an arrow."

She leaned into his shoulder. "All those years I spent on the ranch. . . You and your brothers and sisters were the ones hunting and fishing and horseback riding, but not me. When I wasn't in school, I was reading, but that isn't going to help me raise a teenager or learn how to hunt my dinner."

They had been friends ever since they were freshmen in high school. Her mother had always asked her why they hadn't dated, but she'd never really thought about romance when it came to Levi. They'd just been close friends. He'd dated Chrissy Reed, and she'd spent most Friday nights at the library. But despite Chrissy's jealousy over their closeness, they'd remained friends. They'd also stayed in touch after graduation despite going to different universities, thanks to social media and her infrequent trips back to Shadow Ridge, including after the death of her father three years ago.

Levi McQuaid had grown up in Shadow Ridge, and like her, had been home for the holidays when the Quake hit, along with three of his four siblings. Almost a year later, though, nothing was the same. Levi and his older brother Jace had stepped up as the law in town after their father was shot in a manhunt for a fugitive. Their sister Hope had taken over running the only clinic in seventy-five miles, while Tess, their youngest sister, spent time helping at the clinic as well as with her father's rehabilitation.

If she was honest, though, Josie's struggles weren't the only situation she was concerned about. There had been a number of break-ins over the past few weeks. The community warehouse that stored grain and food was robbed and one of the guards killed. The raids were eventually tied to a gang called the Buffalo Riders, but there were plenty of people out there wanting to take advantage of a vulnerable situation. With very little communication possible with the outside world because of the town's isolated location and the rise of bandits on the road, Jace, who was former military intelligence, had brought on several more part-time officers to join Levi and work under Jace. But while they were all doing the best they could, most of the time, it wasn't enough.

"What are you thinking?" he asked.

"I'm scared because I feel like I'm losing her." Ava slowly exhaled, trying to gather her jumbled thoughts.

"She's lost a lot, Ava. You can't forget that."

"I haven't, but it's no excuse to behave like she is. I need her."

"I could ask Tess to reach out to her. She's not much older."

"That's not a bad idea."

Ava looked up and studied Levi's familiar crew cut and clean-shaven face. He was tough

enough to make it through the rigorous physical and mental challenges of the police academy, and yet there was another side of him—funny, gentle, even vulnerable at times. The kind of man she could always count on. Like today.

"How is Tess?" she asked.

"It's hard to tell. She's quiet, and I always worry about what's going on under the surface. But I've seen her change, in a good way, as she takes on more responsibility. Still. . .like Josie, it's hard."

Ava wiped her cheeks, done with feeling sorry for herself. "These kids need a purpose. To feel needed. And I mean beyond cleaning out chicken coops and weeding the garden. I thought what we were doing was working, but now. . ."

Ava stood and picked the bow and arrow back up. Feeling sorry for herself was never a good idea. "I can keep practicing, but you need to go. You've spent way too much time with me today, though I did think of something positive about today's lesson."

Levi stood, then set his hands on his hips. "And what would that be?"

"We're going to get a pumpkin pie out of this."

He tilted his head. "And you're going to make it?"

"Why am I detecting doubt in your voice?"

"That wasn't doubt, it was. . ."

Levi scratched his chin, apparently searching for a word to describe her less than adequate cooking skills.

"What?" she prodded.

He stepped in front of her and smiled. "I just know that while you are extremely talented, smart, and resourceful—"

"Good save, but my cooking skills are improving. You should have tried my fried chicken this week. It was only a little burnt."

Ava pushed back her shoulders as she spun around to face the target. Stance. Posture. Position. She let the arrow fly and hit the pumpkin dead center.

"See," Levi said. "I knew you could do it."

Ava heard a clatter of hooves and turned around as Gideon Savage rode up behind the house.

"Is everything okay?" Levi asked.

"No, it isn't." Gideon hesitated. "Jace asked me to come get you. Diego Chavez found a body on his property."

ACKNOWLEDGMENTS

So why set a series around the grid going down? A couple reasons. One, I've always loved disaster movies and books. And two, I love exploring how people react, especially when they are forced to work together to survive.

We've lived in Africa for twenty years. I've cooked over an open fire, learned to ration solar energy, and have lived partially off the grid for years. It's a different way of thinking, as it forces you to be creative in using what you have. So this series is pulled partially from my own experiences in order to give my characters a challenging setting. They're going to have to come together to not only fight crime, but to survive.

A huge thanks to Ellen Tarver and Jane Thornton, editors extraordinaire, and Scott Harris for your great insight!

And to my fabulous readers. Ready for another adventure?

AGENTS OF MERCY THRILLERS

USA Today bestselling and award-winning authors Lisa Harris and Lynne Gentry deliver unforgettable and chilling medical thrillers.

Ghost Heart

(Carol Award finalist)

Port of Origin

(Christy-award Finalist)

Lethal Outbreak

Death Triangle

SOUTHERN CRIMES

Despite conflicts that arise between them, the Hunt family is close knit, and when it comes to fighting injustice, they stick together and do whatever it takes to stop that injustice.

Dangerous Passage

(Christy-Award winner)

Fatal Exchange

Hidden Agenda

THE NIKKI BOYD FILES

A string of missing girls that has haunted the public and law enforcement for over a decade. And for Nikki Boyd, the search is personal.

A CBA Best-selling series.

Vendetta

(Christy-Award finalist)

Missing

Pursued

Vanishing Point

STAND ALONE NOVELS

A Secret to Die For

Deadly Intentions

The Traitor's Pawn

US MARSHAL SERIES

The purpose of the US Marshals is to

apprehend the most dangerous fugitives and assist in high profile investigations.

Because if you run, they will find you.

And US Marshal Madison James is one of the best.

The Escape

The Chase

The Catch

MISSION HOPE

Romance and adventure drive this two-book series where a doctor is forced to race against the clock to expose a modern-day slave trade, and with an rebel uprising in play, a refugee camp faces the breakout of a deadly and infectious disease with nowhere to run.

Blood Ransom

(Christy Award Finalist)

Blood Covenant

(Best Inspirational Suspense Novel from Romantic Times)

LOVE INSPIRED SUSPENSE

Deadly Safari

Desperate Escape

Taken

Stolen Identity

Desert Secrets

Fatal Cover-Up

Deadly Exchange

No Place to Hide

The O'Callaghan Brothers Series

Sheltered by the Solider

Christmas Witness Pursuit

Hostage Rescue

Christmas Up in Flames

HISTORICAL

An Ocean Away

Sweet Revenge

To learn more about Lisa Harris and her books, use the QR code above!

ABOUT THE AUTHOR

LISA HARRIS is a USA Today bestselling author, a Christy Award finalist for *Blood Ransom*, *Vendetta,* and *Port of Origin*, Christy Award winner for Dangerous Passage, and the winner of the Best Inspirational Suspense Novel for 2011 (Blood Covenant) and 2015 (Vendetta) from Romantic Times. She has forty plus novels and novellas in print.

She and her husband work as missionaries in southern Africa. Lisa loves hanging out with her family, cooking different ethnic dishes, photography, and heading into the African bush on safari. Visit lisaharriswrites.com to learn more.

Selected Praise for Lisa Harris

"This whirlwind fast-paced chase will please fans of Terri Blackstock." **Publishers Weekly** on *The Chase*

"An excellent thriller with well-drawn characters, and the suspenseful start to Harris' new U.S. Marshals series, this will please fans of Catherine Coulter and J. T. Ellison's Brit in the FBI series." **Booklist** on *The Escape*

"Lisa Harris never fails to bring an action-packed, adrenaline-filled romantic suspense to her readers." **Interviews & Reviews** on *The Escape*

"The Traitor's Pawn by Lisa Harris is full of action, mystery, and suspense. From the first page to the last, Lisa Harris captured my full attention." **Urban Lit Magazine** on *The Traitor's Pawn*

"Lisa Harris has quickly become one of my favorite romantic suspense writers." **Radiant Lit Blog** on *Missing*

"An exciting, well-crafted tale of romantic suspense from veteran thriller-writer Harris." **Booklist** on *A Secret to Die For*

"This whirlwind fast-paced chase will please fans of Terri Blackstock."
~Publishers Weekly

"You don't get it.
I HAVE NOTHING TO LOSE.
That plane crash was a second chance at freedom.
MY WAY OUT."

#TheEscape by Lisa Harris

THE ESCAPE: CHAPTER ONE

There is a razor-thin edge between justice and revenge, where the two easily blur if left unchecked. Five years after her husband's murder, Madison James was still trying to discover which side of the line she was on—though maybe it didn't matter anymore. Nothing she did was going to bring Luke back.

Her pulse raced as she sprinted the final dozen yards of her morning run, needing the release of endorphins to pick up her mood and get her through the day. At least she had the weather on her side. After weeks of spring rains, typical for the Pacific Northwest, the sun was finally out, showing off blue skies and a stunning view of Mount Rainier in the distance. Spring had also brought with it the bright yellow blooms of the Oregon grape shrubs, planted widely throughout Seattle, along with colorful wild currants.

You couldn't buy that kind of therapy.

Nearing the end of the trail, she slowed down and grabbed her water bottle out of her waist pack. Seconds later, her sister, Danielle, stopped beside her and leaned over, hands on her thighs, as she caught her breath.

"Not bad for your second week back on the trail," Madison

said, capping her bottle and putting it back in her pack. She stretched out one of her calves. "It won't be long before you're back up to your old distances."

"I don't know. I'm starting to think it's going to take more than running three times a week to work off these pounds." Danielle let out a low laugh. "Does chasing a toddler around the house, planning my six-year-old's birthday, hosting our father for a few days, and pacing the floor with a colicky baby count as exercise?"

"That absolutely all counts." Madison stretched the other side. "And as for the extra weight, that baby of yours is worth every pound you gained. Besides, you still look terrific."

Danielle chuckled, pulling out her water bottle and taking a swig. "If this is looking terrific, I can't imagine what a good night's sleep would do."

"You'll get back to your old self in a few weeks."

"That's what Ethan keeps telling me."

Madison stopped stretching and put her hands on her hips.

"Honestly, I don't know how you do it all. You're Superwoman, as far as I'm concerned."

Danielle laughed. "Yep, if you consider changing diapers and making homemade playdough superpowers. You, on the other hand, actually save lives every day."

"You're raising the next generation." Madison caught her sister's gaze. "Never take lightly the importance of being a mom. And you're one of the best."

"How do you always know what to say?" Danielle dropped her water bottle back into its pouch. "But what about you? You haven't mentioned Luke yet today."

Madison frowned. She knew her sister would bring him up eventually. "That was on purpose. Today I'm celebrating your getting back into shape and the stunning weather. I have no intention of spending the day feeling sorry for myself."

Danielle didn't look convinced. "That's fine. Just make sure you're not burying your feelings, Maddie."

"I'm not. Trust me." Madison hesitated, hoping her attempt to sound sincere rang true. "Between grief counseling and support from people like my amazing sister, I'm a different person today. And I should be. It's been five years."

"Despite what they say, time doesn't heal all wounds."

Madison blinked back the memories. Five years ago today, two officers had been waiting for her when she got home to tell her that they were sorry but her husband had been shot and pronounced dead at the scene. They'd never found his killer, and life after that moment had never been the same.

Madison shook her head, blocking out the memories for the moment. She started walking toward the parking lot where they'd left their cars. She'd heard every cliché there was about healing and quickly learned to dismiss most of them. Her healing journey couldn't be wrapped up in a box or mapped out with a formula. Loss changed everything and there was no way around it. There was no road map to follow that led you directly out of the desert.

"Did you go to the gravesite today?" Danielle asked, matching Madison's pace.

"Not yet."

She slowed her pace slightly. Every year on the anniversary of Luke's death, she'd taken flowers to his grave. But for some reason, she hadn't planned to go this year. And she wasn't even sure why. She'd been told how grief tended to evolve. The hours and days after Luke's death had left her paralyzed and barely functioning, until one day, she woke up and realized time had continued on and somehow, so had she. She wasn't done grieving or processing the loss—maybe she never would be completely—but she'd managed to make peace with her new life.

Most days, anyway.

"You know I'm happy to go with you," Danielle said.

"I know, but I'll be fine. I'll go later today."

Danielle had been the protective older sister for as long as she remembered.

Her sister took another sip of her water and stared off into the distance. "Want to head up on the observation deck? The view of Mt. Rainier should be stunning today."

"I need to get back early, but there is something I've been needing to talk to you about."

"Of course."

Madison hesitated, worried she was going to lose her nerve if she didn't tell her sister now. "I've been doing a lot of soul- searching lately, and I feel like there are some things I need to do in order to move on with my life."

"Okay." Danielle cocked her head to the side, hands on her hips. "That's great, though I'm not sure what it means."

Madison hesitated. "I've asked for a transfer."

Danielle took a step back. "Wait a minute. A transfer? To where?"

Madison started walking again. "Just down to the US Marshals district office in Portland. Maybe it sounds crazy, but I've been feeling restless for a while. I think it's time for a fresh start. And I'll be closer to Dad."

"Maddie"—Danielle caught her arm—"you don't have to move away to get a fresh start. And there are plenty of other options besides your moving. The most logical one being that we can move Dad up here. I'll help you look for a place for him like we talked about, and we'll be able to take care of him together—"

Madison shook her head. "He'll never agree to move. You know how stubborn he is, besides—he visits Mama's grav every day. How can we take that away from him? It's his last connection to her."

"He needs to be here. You need to be here."

Madison hesitated, wishing now that she hadn't brought it up. "Even if Daddy wasn't in the equation, I need to do this for me. It's been five years. I need to move on. And for me that means finally selling the house and starting over. I've been dragging my feet for too long."

"I'm all for moving on, but why can't you do that right here? Buy another house in a different suburb, or a loft downtown if you want to be closer to work. Seattle's full of options."

Madison's jaw tensed, but she wasn't ready to back down. "I need to do this. And I need you to support me."

"I get that, but what if I need you here? I know that's selfish, but I want my girls to know their aunt. I want to be able to meet you for lunch when you're free, or go shopping, or—"

"It's a three-hour drive. I can come up for birthdays and holidays and—"

"With all your time off." Danielle shook her head. "I know your intentions are good, but I'd be lucky to get you up here once a year."

"You're wrong." Madison fought back with her own objections. "I'm not running away. I'm just starting over."

Danielle's hands dropped to her sides in defeat. "Just promise me you won't do anything rash."

"I won't. I've just been doing some research."

Danielle glanced at her watch. "I hate to cut things off here, but I really do need to get back home. I didn't know it was so late. Come over for dinner tonight. I'm getting Chinese takeout. We can talk about it more. Besides, you don't need to be alone today. I'm sure the anniversary of Luke's death is part of what's triggered this need to move."

Madison frowned, though her sister's words hit their target. "You know I love you, but I don't need a babysitter."

"Isn't it enough that I love your company?" Danielle asked. "I was going to spend a quiet night at home."

"Maddie—"

"I might be your little sister, but I'm not so little anymore.

Stop worrying. I'm good. I promise. I just need a change. And I need you to support my decision."

"Fine. You know I will, even though I will continue to try and change your mind. We could go house hunting together. In fact, remember that cute house we walked through that's for sale a couple blocks from my house? It would be perfect—"

"Enough." She reached out and squeezed Danielle's hand. "Whatever happens, I promise I'll still come up for the fall marathon, so I can beat you again—"

"What? I beat you by a full minute and a half last year."

Madison shoved her earbuds in her ears and jogged away. "What? I can't hear you."

"I'll see you tomorrow."

She flashed her sister a smile, then sprinted toward the park- ing lot. She breathed in a lungful of air. Memories flick- ered in the background no matter how much she tried to shove them down.

For her it had been love at first sight. She'd met Luke in the ER when she went in with kidney stones. He was the hand- some doctor she couldn't keep her eyes off. Ten months later they married and spent their honeymoon on Vancouver Island, holing up in a private beach house with a view of the ocean. As an ER doc and a police officer, their biggest marital prob- lem had been schedules that always worked against them. They'd fought for the same days off so they could go hiking together. And when they managed to score an extra couple of days, they'd rent a cabin in Lakebay or Greenbank and ditch the world for forty-eight hours.

Their marriage hadn't been perfect, but it had been good because they'd both meant the part about for better or worse. They plowed through rough patches, learned to communicate well, and never went to bed angry. Somehow it had worked.

When they started thinking about having a family, she'd decided that she'd pursue teaching criminal justice instead of chasing down criminals after the first baby was born so she could have a regular schedule and not put her life in danger on a daily basis. And Luke looked for opportunities to work regular hours.

But there'd never been a baby. Instead, in one fatal moment, everything they planned changed forever.

Madison's heart pounded as she ran across the parking lot, trying to outrun the memories. Five years might not be enough time to escape the past, but it was time to try making new memories.

Tomorrow, she was going to call a Realtor.

She was breathing hard when she made it back to her car. She clicked on the fob, then slid into the front seat for the ten-minute drive back to the house she and Luke had bought. It was one of the reasons why she'd decided to move. The starter home had become a labor of love as they'd taken the plunge and moved out of their apartment to become homeowners. A year later, they'd remodeled the kitchen and master bath, finished the basement, and added a wooden deck outside. Everything had seemed perfect. And now, while moving out of state might not fix everything, it felt like the next, needed step of moving forward with life.

Inside the house, she dropped her keys onto the kitchen counter and looked around the room. She'd made a few changes over the years. Fresh paint in the dining room. New pillows on the couch. But it still wasn't enough.

No. She was making the right decision.

She started toward the hallway, then stopped. Something seemed off. The air conditioner clicked on. She reached up to straighten a photo of Mount St. Helens that Luke had taken. She was being paranoid. The doors were locked. No one had followed her home. No one was watching her. It was just her imagination.

She shook off the feeling, walked down to her bedroom, and froze in the doorway as shock coursed through her.

There. On her comforter was one black rose, just like she'd found every year at her husband's grave on the anniversary of his death. But this time, it was in her room. In her house. Her heart pounded inside her chest. Five years after her husband's death she still had no solid leads on who killed him or who sent the flower every year. If it was the same person, they knew how to stay in the shadows and not get caught. But why? It was the question she'd never been able to answer.

She'd accepted Luke's death and had slowly begun to heal, but this this was different. Whatever started five years ago wasn't over.

QR code for the series on Amazon!

Made in the USA
Monee, IL
14 December 2022